Between Love and Loyalty

Susannah Hayden

A sequel to *A Matter of Choice*

Heartsong Presents

ISBN 1-55748-503-8

BETWEEN LOVE AND LOYALTY

one

The dark, silky fabric slid through her fingers, oddly cool and empty to her touch. Megan could not remember ever having seen Margaret Barrows wear this dress. With its exquisite hand-tatted white collar, the garment was from an elegant era and seemed out of place in the compact rural stone cottage that its wearer had lived in for the last forty years of her life.

Where would someone who lived out in the middle of nowhere wear such a dress? Margaret had been one of those women who wore practical clothes that would not hinder her physical labor. *There must have been another side to her,* Megan mused, *a side I never saw.*

With a sigh, Megan Browning folded the dress and laid it neatly in the corn flakes carton on the floor next to the couch. The pile of clothes nearly reached the top of the box. Megan sank heavily into the soft beige pillow behind her and surveyed her day's work.

Before they left St. Mary's that morning, she and Stacie Hannaken had stopped at the grocery store for as many flattened boxes as they could fit in Megan's small car. They had reconstructed and filled most of them during the day, and now cardboard cubes towered around her, precarious and mournful. The smell of cardboard mingled with the mustiness of the closed-up house and produced an air almost too heavy to breathe. Megan felt like the walls were closing in on her.

The cottage had been untouched in the four weeks since Margaret Barrows's heart suddenly quit. Margaret had managed to call the paramedics before collapsing, so by the time Megan and Stacie found out she was ill, she was already at the hospital. But they had not even gotten to see her before she died and had no reason to come out to the cottage on a country road forty minutes outside of St. Mary's. A thoughtful farm neighbor two miles away had come regularly to look after the few horses in the camp's stables, but no one had entered the simple home of David and Margaret Barrows, both now gone.

Margaret and David never had children of their own, though they had dedicated their lives to hundreds of children. In the absence of family and at the request of Margaret Barrows's attorney, Megan and Stacie had finally mustered the courage to come to the cottage and sort through the personal items of their friend. Margaret had given them a key months ago, in case of an emergency, but they had certainly never expected to use it for this purpose.

An eerie emptiness greeted them when they turned the key in the lock of the cottage. A half-read magazine lay open on the coffee table, next to a hastily scribbled grocery list and a stack of mail. The bulb in the corner lamp had burned out from being left on so long, as if someone has simply left the room four weeks ago without remembering to flip the switch.

Even after being at the cottage for six hours, Megan felt a hollowness around her as she faced the contradictory tasks of sorting through Margaret's belongings and trying to be respectful of the friend she had lost. Six boxes of usable clothing were stacked by the door, and the seventh and last stood open next to Megan.

Stacie had spent the day wrapping sentimental knick-knacks and filling cartons of books. Megan could hear her, thumping around the bedroom trying to take a quick mental inventory of what else there was to do.

The pictures would have to be next, Megan supposed. She had not been able to bring herself to touch the framed photos covering nearly every inch of the wall across from where she sat. Margaret Barrows was eighty-four when she died; she had known and loved a lot of people over the years and had the pictures to prove it.

It was hard enough to go through her clothing; touching the photos would be like walking on hallowed ground. Margaret went from newlywed to widow in those pictures, with her arms wrapped around dozens of children who had passed through the portals of the Family Homestead in the intervening years.

Shivering, Megan stared out the picture window. Bare trees and gray skies dismally returned her look. The windowpanes had rattled against the bleak wind for most of the day, and now it seemed like wind was blowing straight into the house.

Megan never before had been out to the camp at this time of year. As a child, she had gone to summer camp several times and reveled in an annual burst of independence. The previous spring, when the college and career group from church donated their labor to renovate the camp and open it up again, Megan had been there nearly every weekend, watching winter whimper away and spring break out around her.

But now it was late in the fall, almost Thanksgiving. The temperature dipped more every week, and the invigorated crunch of leaves underfoot was lost in the sogginess left by a week of rain. Spring was but a glimmer of hope at the end of the long tunnel of a Midwestern winter. And without Margaret Barrows, Megan was not sure spring would ever really come to the Homestead again.

"Do you need another box?"

Megan shook herself out of her reverie when she realized Stacie was talking to her. She had not even heard

Stacie enter the room.

"Uh, no, I don't think so," Megan mumbled. She sat up straighter and unconsciously pulled on her characteristic brown pony tail. "I'm just about done with the clothes. How are you coming with the books and things?"

Stacie shrugged one shoulder, discouraged. Her free-flowing rich copper hair rippled with the gesture. "It's tough to know what to do. Some of the books have inscriptions in them that are very personal. I hate to just dump them in a box for the Goodwill. But I don't know what else to do.

"I'm sure Margaret would have liked it if you had some of them."

Stacie grunted a half-laugh. "Brad would have a fit if I carted any more books back to the apartment."

"It seems to me there ought to be some advantage to being engaged to a carpenter," Megan said. "Can't he build you a bookcase?

"Sure, and we'll hang it from the ceiling until he builds me a dream house with a room to put it in." She paused and the sadness in her face deepened. "After Brad and I broke up, Margaret had a lot to do with getting us back together. Now we're getting married next month, and she won't be there to see it."

"I know how much you wanted her to be there," Megan said. "Maybe that elegant dress I just put away was out because she was going to wear it to your wedding."

Stacie forced a smile. "I'd like to think so. She was a classy lady." She swallowed hard. "It just all happened so fast. She wasn't even sick."

"I guess we never thought of her as being as old as she was."

Stacie nodded, holding back tears.

Megan sighed and gestured around the room. "Why did we agree to do this, anyway? We don't even know what's going to happen to this place."

Stacie plopped down in the couch next to Megan. They leaned back, shoulder to shoulder. "The lawyer said it had to be done. I hated the thought of strangers coming in here and going through Margaret's things."

"But why is he being so secretive?" Megan abruptly stood up, agitated. "I know Margaret had a will. Surely she made her wishes known about what to do with the camp. Why is it taking so long to sort out the legalities?"

"She hasn't been gone that long, Megs," Stacie reminded her softly. "I'm sure she arranged for the camp go on like it has for forty years. Someone else will have to run it, that's all. We have to get this place ready for someone else to live in."

Megan picked up a white blouse and folded it for the third time. "I suppose you're right. This is just really hard for me to do."

"I know what you mean. I keep expecting her to bounce through that squeaky swinging door and offer us a pot of tea."

One corner of Megan's mouth turned up a fraction of an inch. "Tea with Margaret; one of the greatest treats in my life."

"I felt really weird when I went through the kitchen a while ago. The copper kettle is sitting on the back of the stove just the same as it always has."

"Stacie," Megan said impulsively, "let's make tea. I want to hear that kettle whistle again."

"Are you sure?" Stacie probed. "Won't it be strange having tea here without Margaret?"

Megan was adamant. "I want to do it. Besides, its chilly in here. You stay here, and I'll fix the tray." Purposefully, she set down the blouse in her hand and turned toward the dining room. When she reached the swinging door that led to the kitchen, she hesitated ever so slightly but then went through it.

Until that moment, she had stayed out of the kitchen because she knew that it was where she would miss Margaret most. But she didn't want to be afraid to miss someone who had been such a unique friend.

The faucet groaned when she turned the knob, and the water, which had not been run for four weeks, spurted out in a brownish color. Megan let it run for a couple minutes, watching it turn clear before filling the copper kettle and reaching for the matches to light the old stove. The gas hissed reluctantly, and the burner finally caught.

Margaret's favorite tea cups sat on a ledge above the stove. Megan took down the two that she and Stacie always used and set them on the table. She did not see the tray out and did not know where to look for it; they might have to do without that nostalgic detail. The sugar bowl was out on the table, but Stacie would want cream, too.

Megan made a face at what the cream would look like after four weeks in the refrigerator. She and Stacie had not touched anything in the kitchen yet; they would have to come back another day for that.

Holding her breath, she opened the door to the refrigerator. A loaf of Margaret's trademark banana bread sat on the top shelf with some odds and ends of vegetables and leftovers below it. Something toward the back looked green and fuzzy. Megan slammed the refrigerator door. Yes, they would have to come back and clear out the old food.

The kettle whistled and Megan turned her attention to making tea. With a cup and saucer in each hand, she bumped the swinging door open with her hip and went back to the living room. Stacie was closing up the last box of clothes.

"Thanks, Megan," she said, taking the offered cup. "I think that about does it for the clothes."

Megan took a sip of the hot tea and immediately felt soothed. "We should have done this hours ago," she said. She negotiated past a stack of boxes and sat down contentedly in the wing chair with the blue afghan slung over the back.

"Well, we've got seven boxes of wearable clothes, four boxes of worn out stuff, twelve boxes of books, ten boxes of knickknacks—and we haven't touched the kitchen yet," Megan tallied. "What are we going to do with all this stuff? Can Brad bring his van out and cart it into town?"

Stacie shook her head. "The attorney said just to pack it up and not to get rid of anything yet."

"Why not? Do they think someone will want these things?"

"I guess just to be safe, we have to leave things here till we know what Margaret's plans were for the property."

"Like who will inherit it?"

Stacie nodded.

Megan's eyes wandered to the wall of photos. "We already know Margaret and David never had children of their own. There are a lot of faces up on that wall, but are any of them relatives?"

"I'm not sure," Stacie said, setting her cup down on the end table and turning to look at the wall. She pointed to one small photo that looked like it was about forty years old. "It seems to me she said once that David had a couple of brothers. I think these kids might be nieces and nephews."

"What's going to happen to this place, Stace?" Megan asked softly. "Who else would care about it the way Margaret did?"

Stacie had no words of comfort to offer against the unknown future of the camp. They had only known Margaret Barrows a few months and had not known her husband at all. Yet their attachment to the camp and belief in Margaret's vision were profound.

Megan shivered again. "I guess I should have worn a sweater. I thought you bumped up the heat a while ago," she said. "It still feels chilly in here to me."

"I turned up the thermostat," Stacie said, "but I haven't heard the furnace blowing."

Megan took a quick sip of tea and set her cup down. She eyed a pile of boxes and decided she could squeeze behind it to the thermostat.

"It's still only 56 degrees in here. That's warm enough for packing boxes, I suppose, but I'm going to go check the furnace anyway."

Stacie raised a questioning eyebrow. "Do you know anything about furnaces?"

"I've lit a few pilot lights in my time," Megan answered confidently.

But she was back after only a few minutes. "The pilot light goes out as soon as I light it," she reported to Megan. "Maybe there's a draft or something; I can't really tell."

"Remind me to have Brad look at it sometime," Stacie said. "Or Dillon. He's pretty handy at keeping the old building in Weston going."

Megan perked up. "Hey, when do I get to come out and see your new office? Won't you be opening the new homeless shelter pretty soon?"

Stacie nodded. "We hope so. I never thought social work could be such an administrative headache. But I think we've got the clearance we need from City Hall in Weston. We're aiming to open January 15."

"Right after your honeymoon," Megan observed. "What does Dillon think of your taking time off right before you open?"

Stacie shrugged. "He's been a pretty good sport. I wasn't sure he even wanted me to keep working for him after I broke up with him and decided to marry Brad after all."

"Have you and Brad decided when to move to Weston?"

"We're looking for an apartment now. Brad's lease is almost up, so he could move into a new place right away. I'll move right after the wedding. Brad has to drive all over the county for his contracting business, but it would make things simpler for us if we lived closer to where I'm working." Stacie grinned at her old roommate and friend. "You know, Dillon is really a great guy, Megan. You really should get to know him better."

Megan waved her hands and turned her face away. "Don't get started on my love life again. I have a good life. I like teaching, I have a great apartment, and if I need something fixed I can borrow Brad from you. What do I need a man for?"

"You really are waiting for a fairy tale, aren't you?" Stacie laughed. "Well, someday your prince will come. Then you'll know why you need a man."

"Have you finished your tea, Madame Psychologist?" Megan mocked. "I'm exhausted. Let's clean up and get out of here."

two

An hour later, tired and hungry, Megan and Stacie pulled up and parked in front of the red brick apartment building Stacie lived in. The neighborhood, usually quiet anyway, seemed to have already settled in for the evening.

The only other activity in the block was a lone paper boy making shadowy deliveries on a bicycle with a dim light strapped to the handlebars. The newspapers, rolled and wrapped in orange plastic, whizzed through the air and thwacked against doors and porches.

The shades in Stacie's apartment were drawn, but muted white light glowed in the windows of her lower level unit.

"Brad must be at your place," Megan said. "At least I hope it's Brad and not some prowler we're about to interrupt."

"It's Brad, all right," Stacie assured her. "He promised to make dinner tonight. You can stay, can't you?"

"Have you ever known me to pass up a free meal?" Megan said, opening her car door.

"Well, sometimes you ask what it is first." Stacie got out, checked the lock and slammed her door.

They walked the few yards to the door. Megan scooped up the newspaper while Stacie turned her key in the lock. As soon as the door opened, they knew what Brad's first ingredient was.

"Onions!" Megan scrunched up her nose. "Don't you think you're going a little overboard?" she called to Brad, who was out of sight in the kitchen.

"And how was your day, Miss Browning?" Brad

responded evenly without interrupting the rhythm of his chopping.

As much as Megan tried to ruffle Brad, she never succeeded. She enjoyed being around Brad and Stacie. Even though they were head over heels in love with each other, and had been for three years, they always made room for her. Even now, just weeks before their wedding, she never felt as if she were in the way. She set her purse down on the end table, dropped her jacket and the newspaper into a chair, and followed Stacie into the kitchen.

"What kind of gruel are you feeding us tonight, anyway?" She peered into a pot that held only simmering water. Brad's dark eyes and hair and friendly face were a welcome sight, but she continued the little game they always played with one another. "So far I see water and onions. I think I deserve better than that after what I've been through today."

"My dear Miss Browning, if you would kindly step out of the way—" He nudged her with his elbow and leaned over her ducked head to kiss Stacie. "How'd it go today?"

Stacie returned his kiss then leaned back against the counter and absently fingered a piece of raw onion. "It was pretty strange, Brad, being at the camp, going through all that stuff."

"I've always suspected that Margaret was a pack rat," said Brad.

"You were right," Stacie answered as she hoisted herself up to perch on the counter next to where he was working. "I felt like we were intruding on something very private."

"Better you than someone who didn't know her."

"I suppose; still, I can think of a lot of ways I'd rather spend a Saturday."

"Me, too," Megan said, opening the refrigerator and

reaching for the orange juice. "And there's still a lot to do. Hand me a cup, Chef Davis."

"Maybe you can get Jenna or Donna or someone else from the group at church to help out," Brad suggested, sliding a plastic cup down the counter to Megan. "Would you hand me that bunch of carrots in there?"

Megan tossed him the two pound bag of carrots. "One more clue. Water and onions and carrots. Sounds delicious." She watched as he pushed the onions aside with the back of the knife and started on the carrots.

"You're as curious as one of your kindergartners, aren't you," he said playfully. He whacked the end off of a thick carrot and tossed it past Megan into the sink. "Do you think you can finish out there in one more day?" he asked, looking at Stacie.

She tilted her head and answered, "Probably, if we got some help. But first we need to know what to do with the boxes we packed today, or there won't be any walking room."

"That lawyer didn't give you much to go on, did he?"

"I'll say he didn't," Megan said, "and I don't like the way all this makes me feel." She poured the orange juice and took a long, eager gulp.

Brad opened the refrigerator again and extracted several celery stalks and a head of cabbage. "Here, if you insist on observing my culinary talents, then at least make yourself useful." He held the knife handle out to Megan and turned to the cabinet behind him. "Where do you keep the rice, Stace?"

"Water, onions, carrots, celery, cabbage and rice," Megan recounted. "It's finally adding up. Chinese!"

"Bingo."

Stacie twisted around to find the rice and handed it to Brad with a measuring cup. "Actually, I'm kind of worried about the camp, Brad," she said. "I'd like to believe

Margaret planned ahead, but it does seem like the lawyer is being awfully mysterious about what is going on."

Brad gave Stacie's hand a quick squeeze before measuring out the rice. "Well, I hate to bring this up, but I heard something yesterday that made me wonder, too."

Megan brought the knife down menacingly hard on the undeserving cabbage. "Out with it Davis," she threatened. "We want the whole truth."

Brad dumped the rice into the pot on the stove and turned the heat down. "I don't really know very much. I got a form letter inviting me to bid on a job down in Grundman County. Somebody wants to put up a set of resort condominiums. It's probably way out of my league—I like to build one house at a time—so I didn't pay much attention at first. But the description of the property sounded familiar." He paused, clearly hesitant to continue.

"What do you mean, Brad?" Stacie prodded.

"It sounded like the Homestead," resuming his efforts with the carrots.

"You can't be serious!" Megan and Stacie said simultaneously. They had not lived together for four years of college without rubbing off on each other.

"I hope I'm wrong," Brad said in his calm way, "but I haven't had a chance to check it out yet."

Megan put the knife down and turned to face Brad. "Do you think you can find out?"

"It should be a simple thing to verify that the property is the Homestead. Finding out who is behind the idea— that's a different matter altogether."

"Doesn't the letter you got say whose project it is?" Stacie asked.

"No," he answered. "The letter is on stationery from some corporation. The information was very sparse, actually."

"Isn't there some way you could find out more?"

Megan asked.

Brad opened an upper cabinet and reached for the wok and a long rubber spatula. "Well, I suppose if I were to show interest in making a bid, I might be able to find out more."

"So what's stopping you?" Megan pressed.

"For one thing, I'm not really interested in the job," he said firmly. "It's much bigger than I'm ready to take on. Secondly, I have plenty of work lined up for the spring already."

"What can it hurt to ask a few questions?" Stacie asked.

"I would be sneaking around under false pretenses."

"Come on, honey, we're talking about the future of the Homestead."

Megan watched the split second of silence between Brad and Stacie and knew that Brad would relent.

"All right," he finally conceded. "I'll ask a few questions to see if I can find out what's behind this. I'll do everything I can short of putting a bid together. But I could be wrong about the property in the first place. Let's not get worked up over things before we have to."

On Monday afternoon, Megan barely got home from Barton Elementary School, where she taught kindergarten, before her phone started ringing off the hook. She dumped her armload of craft supplies in an armchair and grabbed the phone.

"Megan, it's me!"

"What's wrong, Stace?" She was alarmed at the panic she heard in her friend's voice.

"It's true, Megan, it's all true."

"Slow down, Stacie. What are you talking about?"

She could hear Stacie taking a deep breath. "I got a letter today, from the lawyer."

"Margaret's lawyer?"

"Yes. Here, let me read it to you:

> *Dear Miss Hannaken,*
> *I greatly appreciate the assistance you and Miss Browning have been willing to provide in the matter of the old Homestead Youth Camp. Shortly you will receive specific instructions from the new owner as to the disposal of the personal belongings of Mrs. Margaret Barrows.*
> *This is to inform you that Mr. Stanton W. Phillips, the great-nephew of Mr. David Barrows, has been declared the legal owner of the property commonly known as the Old Family Homestead. Mr. Phillips is a resident of the state of California and is interested in the property for investment purposes. It is his intention to develop the property in a more profitable way. Thus, the Old Family Homestead will cease functioning immediately.*
> *If you and your friends have left any personal belongings on the premises related to your activities there in recent months, I advise you to remove them at this time.*
>
> *Sincerely,*
> *Ralph Jorgensen*

Megan groaned and slumped into a chair. "I can't believe that lawyer didn't tell us what was going on. He must have known about this a long time ago." She tried to wiggle out of her winter coat without letting go of the phone.

"We've got to stop this, Megan," Stacie said adamantly. "Can you imagine condos at the Homestead?"

"What can we possibly do, Stacie? Whoever this Phillips guy is, he has more rights to the property than we do according to the law. He's related to David and the legal heir."

"People contest wills all the time," Stacie insisted.

"Stacie," Megan said, trying her best to be sensible, "we're not even legally related to Margaret or David Barrows. Besides, would you really want to go against Margaret's wishes? If she left the property to this nephew, she must have wanted him to have it."

"Come on, Megs," Stacie retorted. "Do you really think Margaret wanted condos to go up in place of that camp? *That* would be going against her wishes."

Megan had to admit Stacie had a point. However, she did not see what legal recourse they had. Stanton W. Phillips now owned that property, and he had every right to put up as many condos as he wanted to.

She blew out her breath and kicked her shoes off her weary feet. "Did you talk to Brad? What does he say?"

"He's still trying to find out who this corporation is. So far he hasn't gotten anywhere."

"Didn't he find out anything?" Megan asked, her disappointment obvious.

"Well, he thinks that the corporation doing this development was set up just for this project. It might be owned by some other group. He just can't tell yet. It could take a couple days to find out."

"Call me as soon as he knows something," Megan said, although she didn't know what difference it would make. "Maybe we'll think of something."

"We have to, Megan. I never even heard Margaret talk about anyone named Stanton Phillips. She would never have gone to so much trouble last spring to get the camp running again if she planned to hand it over to some stranger building condos."

Once again, Megan had to agree with Stacie. "I'd like to think our work was worth something."

Megan heard a click on the line, so she was not surprised to hear Stacie say, "I've got another call. Dillon's out of the office so I'd better take it."

They hung up and Megan sat with the phone in her lap, thinking. She admired Stacie's determination, but was it realistic? A frenzy of emotional energy would not accomplish anything. What they needed was logic—or a miracle—and she was not sure she believed one could happen in this case. The plain fact was that Margaret had left the camp to someone who did not want it, and the people who did want it were helpless to do anything about it.

The days were getting shorter and the room had quickly grown dark around Megan, but she made no move to find a light switch. After a while, her heavy gray cat, Franklin, nuzzled her legs and she lifted him into her lap.

"Well, Franklin," she said, "here we are again. You and me. Two loners keeping each other company."

Franklin twitched his whiskers and gave her a skeptical look. She stroked his back methodically in the way he liked; that was why he had come to her in the first place. He nestled his head in her skirt, content.

"You have such a good life, Franklin," she murmured to the cat. "Somebody takes care of you, comforts you, rubs your back. I know I always tell Stacie I'm happy with my life, but the truth is, I'm a little jealous of hers."

She leaned her head back in the chair and closed her eyes. Megan was very fond of her old cat and enjoyed these moments of quiet. But it was just not the same.

three

Megan jammed the last of her ham sandwich into her mouth and gulped the milk straight from the half-pint carton. Her lunch break was never quite long enough to get her classroom cleaned up and ready for the afternoon session and still have time to eat anything—except the fast way.

Some days she didn't bother trying to eat, but this afternoon she had been hungry. One more glance at the clock told her it was time to go meet the buses and welcome the afternoon students. She smashed the milk carton between her palms and tossed it in the trash as she went out the door.

She took care to button her coat even though she would only be outside for a few minutes. It seemed unseasonably cold; winter was pressing in on St. Mary's with unusual force. Although it had not yet snowed, the temperature had hardly been above freezing for more than a week. The cheerless sky reinforced the grim feel of the frigid air. On days when the wind was blowing, Megan almost believed that some of her smaller students would be carried away in a sudden gust.

The afternoon buses rumbled in right on time. Megan and the other teachers went into a well-established routine, checking to see who was absent, looking for misplaced book bags and stray mittens that might have been left on a bus, and herding the forty-inch-high mass of wiggles into the school building.

Even in the midst of all this activity, Megan noticed a

lone car parked in the far corner of the school's parking lot. Its driver stood leaning against the silver, four-door car, not moving and seeming strangely unaffected by the icy air. Megan was too busy arbitrating minor skirmishes among her students to look closely at him, but she thought it was odd that he was there.

"Karen, no, please don't push Peter." Megan cautioned an exuberant student. "Just wait in line until we're ready to go in."

When she glanced up again, the stranger seemed to focus his stare on the lines forming in front of the school. Slowly, he started moving toward the building. His well-tailored charcoal wool overcoat disguised his body build. The upturned collar hid his facial features. Megan had a strange feeling.

"Pat," she said softly to another teacher, "Do you recognize that guy walking across the parking lot?" She turned to another child. "This way, Tommy. Please stay with the class."

Her colleague swooped up a dropped stocking cap. "No, I don't know who he is. Why?"

"He was there when we came out, just looking at the building. What if he was waiting for kids to arrive?"

"He does seem a bit odd," Pat said. "He's moving so slowly. It's cold out here—I want to get inside as soon as I can."

"We'd better keep an eye out for him later. Don't let him get close to the kids."

She turned to her class, lined up on the sidewalk. "Hello, everybody! We're going to have a great time today. Let's walk—don't run—inside and hang up our coats." She led the line forward, glancing back to be sure everyone followed. Once at the door, she stood aside and counted heads as the children filed by.

Normally Megan was so prepared that she did not have

to look at her lesson plan too often. Today she needed
help focusing, even though she had already been through
the lesson with the morning class. Stacie's news about
the Homestead weighed heavily on her thoughts, and she
had not slept very well the night before. Worry and
fatigue made her feel slightly out of step with most of the
day's activities.

Resolved to do better that afternoon, she picked a bright,
active book about *G*, the letter of the week, and called the
children to sit on their designated X's on the carpet. Her
full denim skirt and practical, loose shirt allowed her to
sit easily on the floor with them. Oblivious to fashion
trends, Megan opted for comfortable clothing whenever
possible, especially at school.

Enthusiastically and distinctly she read the words on
the pages of the book and guided the children through the
motions. During the free play time, she worked on the
bulletin board, trying to put up a seasonal display to show
off the kids' drawings.

From time to time she automatically interrupted herself
to intervene in a dispute or encourage cooperative play
among the children. Then it was time to work on fine
motor skills, and she wrote the letters *A* through *G* on the
chalkboard for the kids to practice copying on their wide-
lined paper.

It was all routine; she had done exactly the same thing
in the morning session for a different twenty-five children. Megan loved her work. Watching her students
develop the skills that would lead to reading in the first
grade was her favorite part. But this particular afternoon,
she was relying on routine and knowing what to do intu-
itively.

At last 3:30 came and it was time to round up the kids
and put them back on their buses. Winter was always a
challenge for kindergartners, with its zippers and mittens

and scarves. Soon enough there would be boots to contend with also.

Outside, Megan looked across the parking lot for the strange silver car. The sky was so gray that the shape of the car nearly faded into the background, but it was there. It had been there all afternoon, apparently. Where was its driver? Was he lurking around the building somewhere, waiting for the kids to come out?

With the children safely on the buses, Megan returned to her classroom to straighten up and try to think what she needed to have ready for the next day. Karen had forgotten her art project on the coat room floor; Megan made a mental note to pay more attention to getting Karen's work into her book bag and to think of some way to help the little girl learn to look after her things.

She picked up a pink plastic vacuum cleaner and set it next to the yellow and white play kitchen. The children had done their best to put the books away, but the shelf needed straightening. She was on her knees, turning books right side up, when she heard footsteps behind her.

"Oh, Miss Browning, you're still here." The voice of Carol Kelley, principal of Barton Elementary, caused Megan to turn around, and, in her crouched position, she nearly lost her balance. "We have a special visitor I'd like you to meet."

Still on her knees, Megan was already staring at the hem of a black wool overcoat. Her eyes wandered up to the collar. Yes, it was the same overcoat. This was the man from the parking lot. The coat hung open casually now, with the collar flattened on the man's shoulders.

Up close, Megan could see that there were flecks of white in the stylish coat, and underneath it, the man wore a double-breasted blue suit. The odd feeling from the parking lot rushed back, but she stood up as graciously as she could and made an effort to be polite.

She put out her hand. "Hello. I'm Megan Browning, kindergarten teacher."

He took one hand from his pocket and returned Megan's grasp. His hand was soft and warm. For the first time, she looked at his face. It was friendly and disarming, with gray eyes and neatly trimmed dark blond hair and a freckle at the tip of his boyish, upturned nose. His mouth spread in an open smile. "Nice to meet you, Megan. I'm Rick Avery."

"Have you been visiting the school today?" Megan asked lamely, knowing that he must have been there all afternoon.

"Actually, I've been trying to visit my sister here," he answered, nodding at the principal.

"Carol is your sister?"

"I'm sorry, Megan," the principal said. "I should make a proper introduction. This is my baby brother, come for a visit at last. I was just giving him the nickel tour of our fine establishment."

"Oh?" Megan raised an eyebrow. "And what finally convinced you to be such a good brother and visit your sister?"

Rick smiled and looked steadily at Megan. "I have to confess, it's a business trip. But if things work out the way I hope they will, I'll be in town quite a bit."

Megan's stomach did a funny flip. There was something very appealing about Rick Avery. Suddenly she felt self-conscious. She was still holding a handful of upside-down books, and she hadn't looked in a mirror since she left home that morning. The clothes that seemed so practical a few minutes ago now felt frumpy.

"Rick, you rascal," Carol said, swatting her brother's shoulder. "You didn't tell me about any business deal in St. Mary's."

"I've been here all afternoon, Sis, and you've hardly

had time to say hello."

"If you had told me you were coming, I could have taken the day off," Carol said in her own defense. "But we have a date for dinner, right?"

"Right," Rick answered his sister, but he was still looking at Megan. She felt awkward and excited at the same time.

Then the intercom squawked and brought her back to reality.

"Miss Browning?" hissed a voice through the speaker.

"Yes?"

"I'm looking for Mrs. Kelley," the office secretary said. "Have you seen her?"

"I'm right here," Carol interjected.

"Good. You have a phone call. It sounds important. Do you want to take it?"

"I'll be right there." Carol turned wearily to Rick and said, "Sorry. I'll be right back and we can finish the tour."

Carol left, which made Megan feel even more awkward. She decided to keep moving. "I was just straightening up. The kids seem to have their own definition of what 'picking up' means."

She knelt at the bookcase again and set the books in her hand at one end of the bottom shelf. "We also made quite a mess with the glitter today."

"Those are some fine looking—and very glittery—*G*'s," Rick said. "Here, let me help." He picked up a stack of construction paper and tapped it against the table to straighten it. "How long have you been teaching?"

Megan smiled to herself and thought *'He wants to know how old I am.'* "This is my second year with my own classroom," she said aloud. "But I did my student teaching here at Barton, too."

"So you've known my sister for three years and she never mentioned you to me?"

Megan turned away in embarrassment. "What's to mention?" she said, trying to take the attention off of herself.

"Give yourself some credit, Miss Browning."

Thankfully, the principal returned at that moment. But she was shaking her head. "I'm sorry, Ricky, but I'm going to have to cancel our dinner. The chairman of the school board wants to see me, and I really can't say no."

Rick didn't seem bothered at all. "I'm sure I'll be fine."

"Tom's out of town for a few days—I wish you had told us you were coming!" she chastised. "But I can give you a spare key and meet you at the house later."

"Sounds great."

"You don't exactly sound disappointed about missing dinner."

"You're the one who pointed out that I didn't give you any warning." He gave his sister a peck on the cheek. "We'll catch up later. Don't worry about me. I'm a big boy."

All during this interchange between brother and sister, Megan had kept herself busy shuffling papers on her desk. When Carol left, she thought Rick would leave, too, but he lingered.

"It was nice to meet you. I hope you and Carol will get your schedules worked out."

"That sounds like you're saying good-bye."

Megan was caught off-guard. "Well, I thought. . ."

"I have perfectly good dinner reservations at the Sunburst Inn. It would be a shame to waste them. Will you join me?"

"I don't know, I. . ." Megan was scrambling for something to say. How could she possibly have dinner with a man she hardly knew—and had been suspicious of until a few minutes ago? She laughed nervously. "You know, I have to confess something. I saw you in the parking lot earlier this afternoon. I was afraid you were lurking around, waiting for one of the children."

"Me? Lurking around?"

"I know it sounds ridiculous, now that I've met you and know who you are. But you were staring and walking in such an odd way."

"I was looking at the building."

"The building?" Megan was puzzled.

"I'm an architect. I look at buildings. I like to look at them from a distance and see how my perceptions change as I get closer."

Megan started to relax and put her things into the canvas bag she carried back and forth to school. "That makes sense. Thanks for explaining."

"So will you?" Rick asked.

"Will I what?"

"Have dinner with me?"

"Yes." She could hardly believe she had said it. The word has snuck out of her mouth against her will. "I'd like to go home and freshen up first."

"I'll pick you up at 5:30."

Megan had always wanted to go to the Sunburst Inn, but she knew the prices were beyond her budget—and the atmosphere too romantic to go without a date.

Rick lightly touched her elbow as they followed the maitre d' to their table in a quiet, cozy corner well away from the busy kitchen. She smiled nervously as Rick pulled out her chair—something that no one had done for her for a long time—and then sat across from her. His smile seemed more genuine and relaxed than hers was. It has been a long time since she had been out on a first date.

The waitress was swift to take their orders; then they were left to wait for their dinner.

"So when was the last time you saw your sister?" Megan

asked as she put her napkin in her lap. She hoped she didn't sound as nervous as she felt.

"Three or four months ago."

"In the summer?"

"Right. We were both home for a few days at the same time."

"Where's home?"

"A little town in northwest Indiana. Our folks still live there."

"Do you enjoy going back there?"

Rick nodded and picked up a bread stick. "Yes and no. It's nostalgic, and I have a couple buddies from high school I see once a year or so. But it seems like another life, another me."

Megan was nodding. "I know what you mean. I grew up in a small town, too. There was a factory nearby, and a lot of people in town worked there. I could have, too." She could feel herself relaxing. "My best friend in high school didn't understand why I wanted to leave and go to college."

"St. Mary's is not exactly the big city," Rick said.

Megan laughed. "True. Maybe that's why I picked it— so I could go to college and still be in a small town."

"I think that's why my sister likes it here, too. It feels like home, but she can be an adult here, instead of always being thought of as somebody's daughter or sister."

Megan smiled and nodded again. "Whenever I go home, I have to listen to my mother's friends say how much I'm like her. Don't get me wrong—I love my mother. But it's nice to be able to be myself and on my own."

"You certainly seem happy with your life."

"I think I am," she answered, stifling the image of another evening at home with Franklin. "How about you? You said this afternoon that you might be staying in St. Mary's."

"I'm trying not to get my heart set on anything yet," he said cautiously, "but it would be nice to be closer to family. That's important to me."

When their meals arrived, Rick and Megan hardly paid any attention to the food. By that point, they were deep into a conversation of childhood memories, family legends, and secret dreams. When the gilded cart full of fancy desserts arrived, Rick suggested they share an enormous piece of chocolate cream pie. They moved their chairs together. Megan had often shared desserts with Stacie; somehow this was different. She looked at Rick shyly several times, hoping that the laughter in his eyes was not because she had chocolate cream on the end of her nose.

To her own surprise, Megan had been able to relax completely with this stranger she had met only a few hours ago. Rick was polite, charming, conversational, interested in her work and family, funny, good looking—flawless as far as Megan could see. She loved being with him and did not want the evening to end. They lingered in the restaurant far longer than they should have considering she had work the next day.

Finally the waitress was giving them irritated looks. They had tied up one of her best tables for the entire evening. The Sunburst Inn Restaurant was getting ready to close. Rick simply smiled and left an enormous tip. He pulled Megan to her feet with a gentle touch and, with his arm around her shoulder, led her back to his car.

When they pulled up in front of her apartment building, he quickly got out and opened her door for her. Holding her hand, he walked her to the entrance of the building, where he turned to face her, still holding her hand.

"I'm certainly glad I ran into you today," he said.

"And I'm glad you're an architect."

"Oh?"

Megan laughed. "I mean instead of someone who just

lurks around school buildings." Reluctantly she turned to put her key in the door. "Do you want to come in for coffee?"

Her heart pounded while she waited for his answer.

"I'd love to, Megan, but it's late, you know. I'll be in enough hot water with Carol for keeping you out this late on a school night."

Megan leaned against the door and nodded at his common sense. "I had a really good time, Rick," she said quietly, looking down at the keys in her hands.

"Me too. I hope we can do it again."

This time she was nodding enthusiasm. "I'd like that."

"I hope you'll like this, too."

Rick caught Megan by the chin and tilted her face toward his. When his lips came down on hers, she knew this was what she had been waiting for all evening. She willingly leaned into his chest to return his kiss.

four

"What about Rosetti's? Don't they sell candles?" Stacie, with three sacks under her arms already, suggested another stop.

Megan had spent the entire morning traipsing after Stacie from store to store in the mall, looking for the details that would make Stacie and Brad's wedding perfect. This was not the first time she had accompanied Stacie on such a venture. To guard against any reluctance Megan might have, Stacie had long ago pronounced that it was Megan's duty as maid of honor to assist in all necessary shopping expeditions.

Normally Megan enjoyed these outings, but she was hot to the point of starting to sweat. If she took off her down jacket, it would be a nuisance to carry. And she was getting tired of looking for candles in a shade of blue she did not believe existed. She had been up late every night that week, and she was beginning to feel the effects. If the right strings were pulled, she could easily become quite crabby.

"Can we just try one more store?" Stacie pleaded. "I promise that after that I'll quit dragging you around."

"Okay. One more store."

Rosetti's, however, was at the other end of the mall. By Megan's calculations, they had walked probably six miles back and forth across the mall already, up the escalators at one end, down at the other end, and back again several times. But she faithfully followed one more time in search of the elusive candles. St. Mary's was too small for a mall of its own, so they had to make the most of the forty-minute trip to a major shopping area.

"I didn't think there would be so much last minute stuff," Megan said, "considering you guys almost got married last spring."

"We never got this close to the wedding date before we broke up," Stacie reminded her. "It's only another five weeks. I promise I'll never put you through planning a wedding for me again. This is it. Brad is stuck with me for good."

Although it was only early November, the mall was already decked out for the commercial holiday season and was becoming more crowded each weekend. Every store window boasted a red and green display, many of them with artificial Christmas trees and manufactured papery snow. The shell of what would become Santa's busy booth was already erected, just waiting for its grand opening on the day after Thanksgiving.

Stacie and Megan dodged rambunctious teenagers moving around in packs and crabby preschoolers in strollers pushed by harried mothers who just wanted to make one last stop before surrendering to the high-pitched demands to go home. Progress was tediously slow, adding to Megan's weary impatience.

"I didn't even know if you were still planning to come shopping with me," Stacie said over her shoulder at Megan who was squeezing through the crowd behind her. "I tried to call you several times, but you never answered the phone."

"I've been busy," Megan explained.

"Every night of the week?"

Megan smiled to herself. She could see Stacie was skeptical of her homebody friend's suddenly busy life. But she answered the question, "Actually, yes."

Megan and Rick had spent every evening that week

together. Some of those evenings they had been at her apartment, but Megan had purposefully left the answering machine on. She had not wanted anything to taint the lovely air of romance blowing through this new relationship. Even the camp's problems had receded to the far corners of her mind.

"Doing what?" Stacie continued her interrogation.

"Stuff."

Stacie stopped abruptly in the middle of the crowd and wheeled around to look at Megan straight on. Her action brought traffic behind them to a halt. As Stacie stood her ground, the crowd parted and reformed after passing them, but not without some disapproving looks at Stacie's impetuous behavior.

"Stacie, you're going to bump into somebody," Megan warned. "Keep going. You're blocking traffic."

Stacie's feet remained firmly in their place. "What's going on, Megan Browning?" she demanded. "What kind of answer is 'stuff'? There's something you're not telling me, and after seven years of being your best friend, I think I have a right to know."

"What about your candles?"

"The candles can wait. Either they have them or they don't. Stop trying to change the subject."

"Let's sit down, then."

Surprisingly, they found an unoccupied bench and sat down quickly.

"Okay, let's have it." Stacie meant business. She did not even put her packages down.

"Remember that prince you said would come?" Megan teased.

Stacie grabbed her arm like a giggling school girl, nearly hurtling her sacks to the floor. "Megan! You met someone and didn't tell me?"

"I'm telling you now, aren't I?"

"Only because I made you." Stacie put her bags beside her on the bench and got comfortable. "Okay, I want the whole story. Don't leave anything out."

"Actually it's a very short story. I only met him on Monday afternoon. He's my principal's little brother."

"What do you mean, 'little brother'?"

"Not so little, really. Pretty big, actually." Sitting alone with her best friend, Megan suddenly let all the wonder and enthusiasm of the last five days flow out. "His name is Rick, and he's absolutely perfect for me."

"Isn't that kind of a drastic thing to say?" Stacie cautioned. "You're that positive after only five days?"

"How long did it take for you to be sure about Brad?" Megan countered.

"One very painful, broken engagement."

"Well, okay, you've got me there." Megan admitted. "But you did finally get back together. Rick is wonderful, Stacie. I want you and Brad to meet him, just not yet. I like having him to myself for a while."

"What does your principal think of all this?"

"I don't really know how much Rick has told her. And it doesn't matter. I can't wait to be with him again tonight."

"Megan, I don't know which side of you to believe," Stacie said, laughing. "A week ago you said you didn't need a man."

"You didn't really believe that, did you?"

"No, not really," Stacie admitted. "You've always been such a hopeless romantic, like when Brad and I split up and you wanted us to get back together."

"Well, you did, didn't you?"

"Okay, you've established that Rick is a living saint. Do you have any plain information about him? What does he do for a living? Does he go to church? That sort of stuff."

"He's an architect. He just left a major firm in Pittsburgh to go out on his own. He's working on some big deal here in St. Mary's. If it works out, he'll open an office here. And yes, he goes to church," Megan said enthusiastically. "That's the most amazing part. I fell for him before I knew anything about what he believed, but we have a lot in common, including our faith."

"So how long do I have to wait before you start answering the phone again?"

Megan laughed. "I promise I'll get back to normal soon." She hiked her purse strap up on her shoulder. "Let's go to Rosetti's and look for those candles."

To their surprise, they found fourteen matching, sixteen-inch tapered candles, in exactly the smoky blue color Stacie was looking for. Stacie insisted that the clerk bundle them up in tissue paper and stack them securely in a box, guarding against any damage before the wedding.

"I'm in the mood to celebrate," Megan said as they left the store. "I'll buy you an ice cream cone."

"We haven't had lunch yet," Stacie protested.

"Don't be so conventional. Come on. What flavor do you want?"

"Well, okay. But I didn't think you'd get so excited about a box of blue candles."

Megan gave Stacie an exaggerated grimace and led the way to the ice cream shop—at the other end of the mall. Comfortably seated, they worked on their double dip cones contentedly for a few minutes.

"Would it spoil your mood if I told you what Brad found out this week?" Stacie asked, swirling her tongue around the edge of her cone in a practiced way.

"I doubt it. Try me."

"Well, we already knew that Stanton W. Phillips inherited the property the Homestead is on. But apparently he's not the one who is doing the condominium project."

"Oh? Is there some hope for the camp?"

Stacie shook her head. "It doesn't look hopeful—but I'm not giving up yet. Apparently Stanton Phillips is looking for a buyer for the property. Margaret and David had the property a long time. I guess it's worth quite a bit of money now."

"The camp may not be a money-maker, but it's doing something important." Megan dabbed a spot of butter pecan ice cream out of the corner of her mouth. "Still, we don't have any right to stick our nose into what the legal owner decides. "

"I refuse to give up that easily, Megan."

"I suppose we could try to contact Stanton Phillips and persuade him to call off the sale. Maybe if he knew more about the camp he'd understand our concern."

"Brad already tried that. Phillips is hiding behind some corporation in Los Angeles and won't take the call. 'Mr. Phillips is not available,'" Stacie mimicked nasally.

"But if he hasn't actually sold the land, then there's still hope," Megan insisted.

"I wish I could believe that, Megs. If you've got some bright idea to try, let me know. But if Phillips won't come to the phone, he won't answer a letter, either." She bit off the last of her cone. "Brad's pretty frustrated. It's hard to deal with an invisible entity two thousand miles away."

"Wait a minute," Megan said, "if Phillips is not the one building the condominiums, why did Brad get an invitation to bid?"

"It turns out it was an exploratory letter. Nothing is certain."

"But who sent it?"

"The developer, I guess. Someone interested in buying the property and seeing what he could do with it."

"Makes sense, I suppose." Megan wiped the evidence of her midday indulgence from her lips. "Maybe Brad could talk to the developer. Is it anyone he's worked with before?"

Stacie shook her head. "No, Frederick something." She scrunched up one side of her face, trying to think. "It starts with an A. Something unusual. Avery. That's it. Frederick Avery."

"Avery?" Megan nearly choked on the word.

"Megan! What's wrong?"

"Are you sure, Stacie? About the name, I mean. Frederick Avery?"

"Megan, why are you reacting this way to a developer you don't even know."

"But I think I do know him.

Stacie stared at her, not comprehending.

"Rick's last name is Avery," Megan said flatly.

Stacie's eyes widened. "You don't think—"

Megan shrugged her shoulders and her eyes filled with tears. "I assumed Rick was short for Richard. But it could be a nickname for Frederick, couldn't it?"

"I thought you said he was an architect."

"He is. But don't developers need architects? And he said he was striking out on his own." She reached into her pocket for a wadded tissue and blew her nose "Oh, Stacie, it's all adding up now. Why didn't I see it coming in the first place?"

"Megs, I'm sorry. I wouldn't have said anything if I had known."

"I had to find out sooner or later, I suppose. And better sooner. Leave it to me to do something as stupid as getting emotionally involved with someone who wants to destroy something I care about."

"You didn't know that when you met him, Megan," Stacie argued. "Give yourself a break."

"What I am going to do, Stacie? The last five days have been perfect, and now, over an ice cream cone, it's all crashing down on me. So much for what we have in common. I didn't even know his full name."

"Let's not jump to conclusions. Look on the bright side." Stacie perked up. "Now we know how to get in touch with the right person about this condominium idea. If Rick feels the same way about you as you do about him, maybe he'll listen to you."

Megan slumped in her chair, wordless. She sniffled and swallowed hard, trying not to burst into tears in the middle of the ice cream shop.

"Stacie, if I bring this up with Rick, he might want to break up. But if I don't and we lose the camp, I'll never forgive myself. Either way I'm going to lose something I care about. How can I choose?"

"Let's just take one step at a time." Stacie was trying hard to be comforting. "Like you said earlier, the sale is not final yet. There's still hope."

Megan tried to hang onto Stacie's words as she moved foggily through the rest of the day. Her anticipation of seeing Rick again that evening had turned quickly from clear joy to muddy confusion. After Stacie dropped her off at home in the middle of the afternoon, Megan sat for more than an hour in the wingback chair, motionless except to rub Franklin's back.

"I know I haven't paid much attention to you lately," she said to the cat. "But it looks like it will be back to you and me keeping each other company again this winter. I hope you'll take me back." Franklin curled his tail as if he understood when the tears finally escaped.

five

As soon as the last child was safely on the bus, Megan ducked back inside her classroom and surveyed the damage done by the afternoon session. On most days, it looked like a whirlwind had been through the room. Today, in anticipation of leaving early, Megan had been more strict about getting things picked up.

Deciding that it did not look too bad, she settled for straightening up her lesson plan book and turning the calendar to the next day's date. While on most days she gladly stayed around the school to get ready for the next day, she was in a hurry to get out that afternoon.

Megan pushed back the sleeve of her oversized shirt to look at her watch. Swiftly, she wrapped her gray coat around her and scooped up her canvas bag. She was on her way to see Stacie's new office. If she left right away, she could get ahead of the rush hour traffic and get to Weston just before Stacie finished work for the day.

At the turn of the key in the ignition, the engine in her old but faithful Toyota sputtered in protest before finally starting. She only hoped the car would make it through the winter; by spring she expected to have enough money saved to get a better one.

Since Rick had been escorting her around town in his late model sedan, equipped with the works, she had become even more keenly aware of what a rattletrap she owned. But despite the way it sounded, the car got her everywhere she needed to go, even after sitting out in the

41

cold all day.

The drive to Weston would take less than an hour, according to Stacie, who had been making the round trip daily for several months. The distance between St. Mary's and Weston, where Brad and Stacie would be moving after their wedding, was only thirty miles, but it was enough that Megan knew she would miss the frequent contact that she and Stacie had enjoyed since being roommates in college. For weeks she had been wanting to get a mental picture of where Stacie worked, and on a lunch hour impulse, she had arranged for this to be the day.

Megan had lived in St. Mary's for seven years. She knew all the shortcuts to the main roads out of town, and on this day, she chose the best one. When she reached the highway, she was relieved to see that Wednesday afternoon traffic was very light, and she merged into the right lane grateful for an excuse to be alone to think. She had found herself becoming impatient with the children in her class that afternoon, which was very unlike her. Obviously, it was time to sort things out.

After finding out that Rick was the developer who wanted to replace the Homestead with condominiums, Megan had seen him several more times. Each time she was caught up in his disarming confidence and tender thoughtfulness toward her, and the conflict raging within her seemed to subside for the time being. But in her mind, Megan knew that ignoring the glaring difference between them was no way to build a solid relationship.

Her feelings for Rick were intense and exciting, but she reminded herself that she had met him less than two weeks ago and there was a lot they did not know about each other. For instance, while Megan was overwhelmed with his attentiveness, she felt no security that he would continue to feel the way he did if she told him that she did not want him to tear down the Homestead.

So far, she had not said anything to him on that subject. But last night he had begun to sense that something was wrong.

"What's wrong, Megan?" he had asked, sneaking up behind her as she made a pot of coffee for the two of them to share.

"What do you mean?" she asked, although she already knew.

"You don't seem to be yourself tonight." He put his hand on her waist.

She moved away from him quickly and reached for the sugar bowl.

"Don't you feel well?" Rick asked.

"I'm perfectly fine," Megan answered, trying to sound sincere. She laughed briefly. "Maybe I'm just exhausted from all this late night activity. I'm not used to it, you know."

"You'd better get used to it," Rick said. "If I have anything to say about it, there will be many more late nights."

He had reached for her once again, and this time she had not resisted. Her head told her one thing; her heart said something else every time he touched her.

Megan flipped on her turn signal and glanced in the mirrors for traffic to her left. Trapped behind a slow-moving truck, she was losing precious time. Besides, she hated not having a view of the road ahead of her. She pulled smoothly into the passing lane and picked up speed. The road before her was clear, but the horizon turned more gray each moment as the clouded winter sun completed its duty for the day. It would be dark before she reached Weston.

There was no true urgency about seeing Stacie's office. It certainly would have made more sense to make the drive to Weston on a day when she could have started out earlier. By the time she arrived, it would be almost time for

Stacie to pack her briefcase and head back to St. Mary's herself. But Megan had felt like taking a drive, and visiting Stacie seemed like the best excuse she could come up with to do it. Maybe she could persuade Stacie to stay and have an early dinner in Weston before heading back.

Arriving at the city limits of Weston, Megan fished in her coat pocket for the directions she had jotted down during her phone conversation with Stacie at lunch time. *Go four-tenths of a mile past the city limit sign to second stop light, turn left, two blocks down, third building on the right.*

The directions proved to be exactly right—which was no surprise to Megan; Stacie was precise about most things. Five minutes later, Megan parked in front of the old building that Dillon and Stacie had remodeled into a homeless shelter on a downtown street. The two-story red brick building had large inviting windows on the front wall and a sign promising that the shelter would be "opening soon."

Stacie and Dillon had hoped to be open in the fall, before the winter months began, but there had been more work to do on the building than they had anticipated. The deepening chill in the air made Megan shiver and reminded her that the upstairs sleeping rooms the shelter would provide were badly needed.

Megan looked up to see Stacie poking her head out the front door of the building.

"There you are," Stacie said, "right on time."

"I left my classroom a mess," Megan said, taking the short steps quickly, "but I didn't want to keep you waiting."

Stacie smiled and held the door open. "Come on in. I'll give you the tour, no charge."

The building had once held offices and a warehouse, so part of it was divided into smaller rooms where Dillon and Stacie had their offices and where a receptionist and other staff would work once the shelter opened.

At the rear of the building was a large room that had been converted into a dining hall to seat about sixty people at a time. The former offices on the second floor had been reconstructed into eight sleeping rooms and two large bathrooms.

"This place looks great," Megan said enthusiastically. "What do you have left to do?"

"Some of the rooms upstairs have not been painted," Stacie said as she led the way back to her office, "and the plumbing in the second bathroom is not finished."

She took Megan's coat, hung it on the back of the door, and gestured that they could sit down. "We're also still waiting for some donated dishes and commercial size pots before we would be ready to serve meals. But the biggest hold up is that we still have one more hoop to go through with the city council, and that can't happen until they meet during the third week in December."

"That's too bad," Megan said. "It's really getting cold out at night these days."

Stacie nodded. "I know. Dillon's been trying to get permission to at least let people come in and sleep on the floor, just to get out of the cold, but so far he hasn't gotten anywhere."

"I hope he can work something out before long."

"Dillon is a go-getter. We would never have gotten this far along without the energy he puts into this place." She paused and shuffled the files on her desk in a distracted way. "I only wish he could work a miracle on the Homestead, too."

Although they had not verbalized it, both Stacie and Megan knew that their shock and grief about the camp's future was what had brought them together that afternoon.

"Did I hear my name?"

Stacie and Megan looked up to see Dillon standing in the doorway.

"It's nice to see you, Megan. I hope Stacie is not telling you mean things about me behind my back," he said, running his fingers through his curly blond hair. He had a comfortable, rumpled look, a physical image that did not project the efficiency of his work.

"Quite the contrary, I assure you" Stacie said.

"She's singing your praises," Megan added, sounding more cheerful than she felt. "I can see by the looks of this place that she's telling the truth."

"I didn't mean to be eavesdropping, " Dillon said, changing his tone and the subject, "but I heard you say something about the Homestead. The two of you look pretty down in the dumps about something." He leaned casually against the door frame and looked from one to the other, questions springing from his eyes.

"It's a long story, Dillon, but it looks like the Homestead may not be here much longer," Stacie explained.

"I remember you told me that Mrs. Barrows died recently."

"That's when it all started. Apparently she left the property to a great-nephew of her husband, and he doesn't care about the camp. Her lawyer tells us that the nephew is planning to sell the land." Stacie glancing at Megan. "And there's already a developer interested in putting up condominiums."

Megan was grateful that Stacie did not supply Dillon with the rest of the story—that Megan had so quickly become attached to the developer himself.

Dillon winced and plunged his hands into his pockets. "That doesn't sound good. I really admired what you all did out there last summer. And Stacie, I know you were hoping that next year some of the kids from the shelter could go to camp on scholarships."

"I'm still hoping that," Stacie insisted. "As far as we know, nothing has been finalized. Anything could happen."

Dillon nodded his appreciation of her positive attitude. "Let me know if there's anything I can do to help."

"Thanks, Dillon," Megan said, "but I'm sure you have plenty of headaches of your own just trying to get this place open."

Dillon was shaking his head. "No, I'm serious. That camp is a worthwhile thing. I know I'm not part of your church group, but I'd love to help out in some way."

Megan and Stacie glanced at each other at this unexpected offer of help. "Thanks, Dillon," Stacie finally said, "we'll keep that in mind."

Dillon locked his fingers together and stretched his arms straight out in front of him. His knuckles cracked with the motion. "Well, I've got some work I have to get done before I can go home, so I'd better get back to it." He turned to Megan. "It was nice to see you again, Megan. Don't be a stranger around here."

He left them alone. Instinctively, they listened to hear his footsteps recede down the hall before resuming their conversation.

"Well, that was nice of him," Megan said.

"I'm sure he means it, too," Stacie added. "If I thought there was anything he could do, I wouldn't hesitate to ask."

They sat, wordlessly sharing the futility of the moment. Stacie broke the silence with the question that hung in the air between them.

"How's Rick?" She asked simply.

Megan looked away, awkwardly. "He's fine."

"Are you still seeing so much of him?

Megan nodded.

"I hope you know what you're doing," Stacie said.

Megan laughed nervously. "Of course I don't know what I'm doing. Good old sensible Megan, dating a man who wants the opposite of what she wants. Makes perfect sense, doesn't it?"

"I just meant that I don't want to see you get hurt, Megs," Stacie said gently.

"I'm afraid I'm going to get hurt either way."

"Let's grab some dinner together and talk about it."

"I was hoping you would say that," Megan said, relieved.

It was late when Megan got home. The apartment was dark except for the light in the living room that went on automatically at six o'clock every evening. Franklin greeted her with a resentful purr and rubbed himself against her legs. She scooped him up and scratched behind his ears.

"How are you, Franklin? It's been a long day, hasn't it?" She threw her coat over the back of the couch and went into the kitchen to check the cat's food and water. On her way past the phone, she hit the button that would play back her messages.

"Megan, it's me," said Rick's voice. "I hope you had a great time with your friend tonight. I just wanted to tell you I missed you and I'm looking forward to seeing you tomorrow. Sleep well. I love you."

The machine beeped to signal the end of the message. Megan stopped in her tracks, an open can of cat food poised in the air, and turned to stare at the machine. With her heart pounding, she walked back to the phone and listened to the message again, especially the last words.

Yes, she had heard him right. But did he really mean those words?

six

"Franklin, get off the couch."

Megan nudged her faithful feline friend down to the floor. She sat where Franklin had been, in the center of the couch, and gathered up the evidence of spending her free Saturday afternoon cutting snowflakes for the bulletin board at school.

Despite her best effort, snippets of white construction paper dribbled behind her when she took the scraps to the trash in the kitchen. She had vacuumed the apartment earlier in the day.

"When will I learn," she said aloud when she saw the trail of white, "to make my mess first and clean up last?"

Franklin arched his back and stared at her. He was not happy with being displaced so she could clear up the clutter.

Megan stooped to pick up bits of snowflakes gone awry. Crushing the scraps in one fist, she used the other hand to tickle Franklin's chin. "Sorry, Franklin. I didn't mean to yell at you." Franklin gave no response. "Oh, well, go ahead and pout, then."

Megan stood up and looked around. Despite the snowflakes, the apartment looked fairly tidy—not that it mattered. Rick had already seen her place several times, so she did not feel pressured to impress him.

She lived in the upstairs unit of a two-flat building that was close to a hundred years old. The way the rooms were laid out one behind the other was a bit odd, the plumbing creaked and rumbled, and she had to be careful not to run too many electrical appliances at the same time.

Now that she had been teaching for several years, she could probably afford to move to a nicer apartment in Stacie's neighborhood on the other side of town, but Megan was comfortable in the old building, and it was close to the school where she taught. The landlord had let her paint and wallpaper to her own tastes, and she was content.

The gray striped couch faced a brick fireplace that had warmed her winter evenings for the last three years. Already Rick and Megan had curled up in front of the fireplace several times, watching the flames as an excuse to be mesmerized by their feelings for each other.

Twin white bookshelves on either side of the fireplace unashamedly showcased her continuing interest in children: educational theory textbooks, craft ideas and random supplies, a collection of vivid illustrations, a scrapbook from her student teaching. Miscellaneous crayons and markers poked out from behind piles of loose paper.

Megan looked at the clock on the mantle and saw that it was time to get dressed. Rick would be there in a few minutes to pick her up for a movie.

The nervousness of the last few days had left her without an appetite, but she knew she would get a headache later if she didn't eat something soon. Reluctantly, she shuffled into the kitchen and spotted a jar of peanut butter on the counter. She stuck a tablespoon in the jar and pulled out a generous portion. Eating straight from the spoon, she padded to the one small bedroom tucked away behind the kitchen and opened the closet.

The clothes that were so comfortable to teach in somehow did not seem right for going out with Rick. It was only a movie, but she wanted to get out of the jeans she had been in all day, and she knew Rick would be freshly dressed, probably with another of his many colorful sweaters. She inspected the options and with a resigned sigh decided on a pair of black twill slacks and a soft, pale pink sweater.

Looking in the mirror, she scowled and shook her head. Her problem, she thought, was that she was so nondescript in her appearance. She had no striking hair color to show off like Stacie's copper penny hair, just mousy brown hair that was a little on the thin side, usually pulled away from her face in a casual pony tail. Her eyes, also brown, were just eyes, no glimmer of hidden beauty, no spark of wit, no mysterious passion. Standing before her dresser, she convinced herself that Rick was going to get tired of her pretty soon anyway.

She yanked the clip away from her neck, letting her hair fall free, then grabbed a brush off the dresser and started pulling it through her hair with short quick strokes. Why was she feeling this way? Was she nervous because Rick was coming to pick her up? A week ago she had not thought anything could spoil her mood when she was with Rick. Now she was not so sure.

A pink ribbon was already twisted around her fingers when she decided to leave her hair loose. Maybe she would look less like a kindergarten teacher and more like a woman in love, she thought, if she left her ponytail behind for the night. She looked around for her spoonful of peanut butter and finished it off before going into the bathroom for some fresh lipstick.

While she was in there, trying to make her mouth look less ordinary, the doorbell rang. Rick had arrived.

The movie ended a few minutes after ten. Megan and Rick stayed in their seats, his arm around her shoulder and the empty popcorn box in her lap, until the very last credit had rolled off the screen and the last deep note of the sound track had faded away. Finally they stood up and ambled up the aisle. When Rick squeezed her shoulder, Megan quickly responded by putting her arm around his waist and leaning her head against his chest.

Halfway out to Rick's car, he broke their comfortable silence. "I have a surprise for you, Megan."

She looked up at him. "What is it?"

He smiled and shook his head. "Then it wouldn't be a surprise."

"I'm no good at surprises," she said in a false pout. "Tell me."

"Uh uh. But trust me, you'll like it."

He opened the car door for her and in cavalier fashion gestured that she should enter. As she sank into the deep cushion of the front seat, she couldn't help thinking of the broken springs in the seats of her own car. Everything about Rick was different from her, yet all she wanted was to be with him.

They pulled out of the parking lot and Rick smoothly steered the sedan out into traffic. As he did so, he popped a tape into the tape deck, and the car filled with the strains of Pachelbel's *Canon*. Megan leaned her head back against the headrest and closed her eyes, caught up in the interweaving of the melodies.

When she opened her eyes a few blocks later, she was startled. "Hey, where are we? You missed the turn off to my apartment."

"That's the surprise."

"What's the surprise?" She was still baffled.

"We're not going to your apartment. We're going to mine."

Her heart seemed to leap and sink at the same time. If Rick had taken an apartment, it meant he planned to stay in St. Mary's. But it also meant that the deal with Stanton Phillips must have gone through.

"An apartment?" she said, blinking her eyes. "You're not staying with your sister anymore?"

Rick shook his head, smiling. "Nope. I found a furnished place that I really like. Actually, I'm subletting it temporarily till I'm more sure about my plans."

He paused to laugh a little. "Carol is great as far as sisters go, but there's no point in wearing out my welcome. Besides, I wanted a place where I could take you to be alone. I don't want you to feel like you always have to entertain me at your place."

Megan reached out and put her hand on his knee. "I love having you at my place."

"Well, I'm not so sure that cat of yours likes it."

"Franklin? He just likes to pout." Megan said, amused. "But having your own apartment will be great. I can't wait to see it."

"Your timing's perfect. Here we are." He turned into the driveway of a new apartment building. Megan had driven by the complex several times and wondered what the apartments were like. Now she could find out. They quickly walked through the lobby and up the elevator to the fourth floor.

Rick turned the key in the lock of his apartment, situated just across from the elevator, and pushed the door open. "Welcome to my humble abode," he said dramatically.

Megan walked in and surveyed the spacious apartment. The living room, at least twice the size of her own, had bright white walls with oversized prints by contemporary artists splashing color on the walls. Soft, black leather furniture with chrome trim was grouped in one corner around a glass-topped coffee table. The entertainment center held a large television and a fully-equipped stereo system. A deep maroon rug and accent pillows added a touch of warmth to a relatively spartan room.

Slowly turning around in a small circle, Megan tried to absorb what she saw. In the car Rick had said he really liked this place—but it was completely different from anything she would choose.

She could appreciate the sense of taste that had gone into planning it and could speculate on the artistry that would appeal to an architect, but she was so used to her functional, crowded, two-flat unit that she could not imagine living in a place like this. Was this what Rick wanted to put up on the camp land—a stark, metal structure that only the wealthy could afford to live in?

"What do you think?" Rick asked, his enthusiasm obvious.

"It's very modern," Megan answered quickly, glad to find a word that was honest without revealing her emotions.

"I know it's different from what you're used to, and if it were really my own place, I'm sure I would change some things. But I think I'll be comfortable here until I know whether I'll be able to stay in town."

Megan swallowed and asked the question she had been avoiding for several days. "How is your big deal coming along?"

Rick shrugged one shoulder. "Not as well as I would like, but I'm still very hopeful. There's some legal technicality about the title that has to be cleared up because the owner just inherited it, but we're already working on the details of the deal. And of course, there's always the outside chance someone one else will make a better offer, but I'm not too worried about that."

He touched her elbow and guided her across the room.

"Here, let me show you something."

Before her on a white dining room table was an architectural model of a small group of buildings. "Is this your project?" she asked, although she already knew the answer.

"This is it! Look, there will be eight units here and another four over here, across from the tennis courts. I can design them with either two bedrooms or three, with a lot of custom options."

He bent his head closer to the model to inspect the detail once again. "My main interest is the outside, of course. I plan to use archway entrances. See how the roof angles over here?"

He continued talking and pointing, sometimes bending low over the model to examine an intricate detail, and glancing back up at Megan to share his excitement. She nodded and smiled at what she hoped were appropriate places. The truth was that most of what he was saying was lost in a dizzy blur of emotion. She was flushed, and despite the expanse of the room, she could hardly breathe. Finally, she could take it no more.

"Rick, we need to talk," Megan said, interrupting Rick's flow of enthusiasm. Seeing the model there on the table made it impossible to bury the issue any further.

"What's the matter, Megan? Don't you like the model?"

"It's great, Rick," she assured him. "It looks like a wonderful place to live. There are just some things I need to clear up." She glanced at the couch. "Can we sit down?"

They sat on the couch, but Megan twisted so that she was facing Rick with several feet between them.

"Rick," she began, "when we met you said you were an architect and that you were working on a big deal that might make it possible for you to move to St. Mary's. My friend, Brad—remember I told you he's a contractor?—

heard about a project out in Grundman County, and I think it might be the same project."

"It could be," Rick affirmed. "I'm trying to buy land in Grundman County that has some rundown buildings on it. It's sort of a ranch or camp."

"The Old Family Homestead," Megan supplied.

"You know the place?" Rick was surprised.

Megan fingered the cording on what she was sure was an expensive throw pillow. "Yes, I know the place. I went to camp there several times when I was a kid." She paused and tried to keep the tremble out of her voice. "Then last spring Brad and Stacie and a bunch of us from church helped to spruce the camp up and get it open again."

"I heard something about that from the real estate agent. And I have to admit, it didn't look too bad when I was out there a few weeks ago. I could tell someone had been working on it."

"We put a lot of work into it last spring, and we had over two hundred campers during the summer weekends. We were hoping to run camps during the week this year."

"But the buildings are old, Megan; they really are ready to be torn down. What I'd like to do will be so much nicer."

"Nicer for whom?" Megan challenged. "Those kids who can't afford to go off to some expensive summer camp— it won't be nicer for them."

Rick was silent for a moment, then said, "I guess I see what's been bothering you lately. Since I haven't known you very long, I wasn't sure which was the real you—the way you were the first week we met, or the way you've been the last few days."

"I'm sorry, Rick," Megan said. "I haven't meant to be withdrawn. I just didn't know what to say to you. You're so enthusiastic about the project. It's your dream, and I care about you enough to want your dreams to come true. But why does it have to be on that land? Why does the camp have to be sacrificed?"

Rick stood up and took a few steps away from the couch. He sighed deeply. "Megan, it's an old camp. I'm sure it has a wonderful, colorful history and thousands of kids have loved going there, but it's time for something new. I looked at those buildings, Megan. They're very quaint, but some of them don't look so safe to me."

"They can be fixed. That's Brad's line of work."

"It would take an enormous infusion of money to modernize that old place and keep it running as a camp."

Megan could feel her temper rising. "Please don't refer to the Homestead as 'that old place,'" she said with an even tone that did not reveal the emotion welling up inside her. "Not everything has to be modern in order to be worth something!"

"No, of course not," Rick was quick to agree. "Look, Megan, you know this is an opportunity I've been waiting years for. The plain fact is that Stanton Phillips wants to sell that land, and he's willing to let me have it for a price I think I can afford. If I don't buy it, some big city developer will come along and snatch it up, and the camp will still be gone."

Megan choked back her tears. "I know," she said hoarsely. "But I'm not in love with one of those big city developers."

"And you are in love with me?"

Wordlessly, she nodded.

Rick sank back into the couch and enfolded her in his long arms.

"Please, Rick, promise me you'll think about it," she murmured into his chest. "Please think about trying to save the camp."

Rick smoothed the hair on the back of her head. "Shhh. Yes, I'll think about it. Let's calm down. I just have one more thing to say."

"Yes?"

"I love you, too, Megan Browning."

She turned her face up to meet his kiss as his hands moved over the contours of her back and shoulders and they sank into the soft, black leather cushions.

seven

"Did anyone check the turkey?" Megan asked, stooping to peer through the glass oven door in Stacie's kitchen.

"Just jiggle the leg," Stacie called from the other room, where she was setting the Thanksgiving table for eight. "If it feels loose, then we could take the turkey out."

Stacie appeared in the doorway, with a stack of plates in her hands. Megan cautiously opened the oven door and wiggled the turkey leg with her fingertips. "How loose is loose?" she asked.

"I think it's done," Stacie said, glancing at the clock. "After all, I got up at the crack of dawn to put it in."

"Let's get it out of there, then." Armed with large blue potholders, Megan pulled out the oven rack and lifted the roasting pan to the counter. "Now what do we do?"

"Just let it cool off for a few minutes," Stacie instructed.

"Shouldn't everyone be here soon?" Megan asked. She indulged in a deep whiff of the turkey aroma.

"Donna called a few minutes ago. She and Paul are on their way. And Dillon is always prompt."

"And Jenna?"

"I'm sure she'll be here soon."

"It was really nice of you to invite her, Stacie," Megan said, "considering she has a crush on Brad."

Stacie waved the thought away. "That's over and done with. Jenna spent a lot of time taking care of Mrs. Barrows and worked very hard at the camp last summer. She's not really the flake I thought she was. Besides, I remember what it's like to be a college student stranded at the holidays." She changed the subject. "Now what about Rick? I hope he's coming."

"Yes, he's coming." Megan twisted a potholder absently between her fingertips. "I have to confess, I'm a little nervous."

"Well, you've certainly kept him hidden from the rest of us. Brad and I are anxious to meet him."

"Just don't interrogate him."

Stacie gave a mock gasp. "Me? Interrogate the man who has swept my best friend off her feet? Whatever were you thinking?"

Megan blushed and threw the potholder at Stacie. "Come on, Stace. I want this to be a nice day."

Stacie straightened her expression and turned back to her table setting. "Okay. We'll play it by the book today. Can you get down the good glasses? They're above the refrigerator."

Just then the door opened and Brad walked in, laden with last minute items from the grocery story. "Smells great in here!" he said, taking a deep breath of the holiday air.

Stacie took the paper sack from his hands. "Thanks," she said. "I can't believe I forgot to get whipped cream for Thanksgiving."

Brad chucked. "I feel sorry for people working on Thanksgiving, but we weren't the only last minute shoppers in town."

The doorbell rang, making Megan jump involuntarily. Rick had cheerfully agreed to have Thanksgiving dinner with the group at Stacie's, although his sister was expecting both Rick and Megan for dessert later. Megan was nervous about the whole day. When the doorbell rang, the glasses in her hand rattled against each other.

Brad reached behind himself and opened the door. "Paul,

Donna, come on in. Let me have your coats."

Donna shivered as she handed her coat to Brad. "It's really turning into winter out there. I'm already looking for spring to come."

"You've got a long wait," Paul warned, handing his coat to Brad also. "Jenna's just behind us. Who else is coming?"

"Dillon Graves—the guy I work with—and a friend of Megan's," Stacie answered simply and naturally. Then she swiftly changed the subject. "Paul, there's a chair in the corner of my bedroom that we're going to need. Can you get it, please? Brad, I could use some help in the kitchen."

Brad rubbed his palms together eagerly. "I am at your disposal, mademoiselle."

Megan and Donna finished setting the table just as Jenna arrived. When the bell rang, Megan answered it, hoping it would be Rick. As she welcomed Jenna, she could not help looking past her through the open door to see if he was in sight.

Why hadn't she asked him to come earlier? she chastised herself. It would have been easier to introduce him to Stacie and Brad first, before the others got there.

As the others drifted toward the kitchen, everyone with a different opinion about how the turkey should be carved, Megan hung back in the living room, anxious and insecure. Rick was so likeable, it was hard to imagine that the others would not warm up to him just as quickly as she had. But she wanted to get past that awkward moment of first introductions.

Although Stacie had promised not to embarrass Megan, she knew Stacie would be watching Rick closely. After all, she had done the same thing when Stacie first met Brad. At the core of their friendship was the instinct to look out for each other.

Megan listened to the sounds coming from the kitchen: Brad insisting that he knew how to carve a turkey but asking what knife he should use, Donna mashing the potatoes, Stacie characteristically making sure everything was running smoothly.

The doorbell rang again. "I'll get it," Megan called out.

It was Dillon, not Rick. "Oh, hi, Dillon," she muttered.

Dillon laughed awkwardly. "Thanks for the warm welcome."

Megan felt her face redden. "I'm sorry, Dillon. I thought it would be someone else."

"Sorry to disappoint you."

Megan scrambled to get out of the hole she was digging. "I didn't mean it that way." She reached for his coat. "Here, let me hang that up for you. The others are in the kitchen."

"Obviously not everyone. Who was I supposed to be?"

Megan smiled nervously. "I invited a date, if you must know. You haven't met him before."

"You're certainly making me curious, the way you're behaving."

Megan gave Dillon a push toward the kitchen. "I'm sure there must be something they need you for in there."

Dillon responded good naturedly. "I can tell when I'm not wanted."

He disappeared into the already crowded kitchen. Megan heard the others welcoming him as she pushed aside the curtain to look out the window, hoping to see the familiar sight of Rick's gray sedan. Too nervous even to focus properly, she finally spotted it across the street; Rick was just getting out. Megan didn't wait for him to ring the doorbell. When he got close, she opened the door and pulled him in, wanting a moment alone with Rick before she had to share him publicly.

She welcomed his kiss and fleetingly wished that they were spending the whole day alone together.

"You look great," he said, letting her take his coat. He looked around the apartment. "This is a nice place. Your friends have good taste."

Megan linked her arm through his. "Let's go in the kitchen. I'll introduce you to everyone."

Twenty minutes later the group was assembled around the dining room table, waiting for Brad officially to present the seventeen-pound turkey, glazed and golden on a white china platter. Proudly, he set it down at the head of the table, amid the oohs and ahs of the rest of the group. He leaned over to kiss Stacie. "Everything looks great, honey."

Megan looked up at Rick and saw the same expression in his face that she saw in Brad's. At that moment she was sure that Rick loved her the same way Brad loved Stacie. She choked back a wave of emotion. This was one Thanksgiving when she was truly grateful.

"Stacie and I are glad you could all be with us today," Brad said, speechlike. "In a few weeks, we'll be married, and we hope that you'll all be with us on that special day, too. Let's give thanks." He closed his eyes and everyone followed his cue.

"Lord, we come to You humbly and gratefully, knowing that every good thing that we have has come from You. One day a year cannot not possibly be enough time to express our thanksgiving for the blessings we enjoy and that we too often take for granted. But receive our sincere thanks for the gifts of friendship and love and the people whom we cherish. Bless our day together, making us mindful of Your generosity toward us when we least deserve it. In Jesus' name, Amen."

Megan smiled again at Rick and started passing dishes

around the table. Brad was busy carving the turkey, taking requests for light and dark meat. The mashed potatoes, dressing, cranberry sauce, vegetables, and steaming rolls slowly circulated, and plates were heaped high with what was only the beginning of holiday overeating.

"The eating season has officially begun," Paul said, methodically dribbling gravy over the mound of potatoes on his plate. "I'll start today and not stop until New Year's."

"That's what the holidays are for," Brad offered, dropping some white meat onto the plate Stacie was holding out. "It's an American tradition. And in the Midwest, we consider it a consolation prize for having to endure winter."

"You can say that again," Donna agreed, reaching for the butter. "I grew up in Florida, and even though I've been here eight years, I never get used to this dreary, miserable weather."

"Well, I assure you, summer will come," Dillon said. "The sun *will* shine again. Can I have the salad, please?"

"Summer won't be the same without Margaret Barrows," Jenna said quietly. "I really miss her."

For a moment, the whole group was silent, everyone except Rick wordlessly agreeing on their sense of loss.

"She would hate what's happening now," Donna said, shaking her head. "What's happening to the camp is awful."

Megan stiffened and groaned inwardly. Why couldn't everyone just enjoy the holiday meal? If the conversation proceeded much further along this line, Rick would certainly become uncomfortable. Brad and Stacie knew about Rick's involvement with the camp property, but the others did not.

Paul took his cue from Donna as smoothly as if they had rehearsed it. "These big development corporations think they can just barge in and do whatever they want, no matter who it hurts," Paul said. "It's about time someone started standing up for some decent values."

Megan caught Stacie's attention and pleaded with her eyes for her friend to do something to prevent what was happening.

"I think the best part of holiday eating is the pies," Stacie said with artificial brightness. "We've got three kinds today. Megan made them."

But it was too late to change the path of Paul's rampage. "I mean it," he continued as he slathered butter on his bread. "We're sitting here eating too much, talking about American holiday traditions. Well, there are some other American traditions, too, and I think they're worth fighting for."

Megan looked frantically from Brad to Stacie. *Please, oh please, do something!* her eyes cried out.

"Maybe we should check with city hall," Donna suggested, "to see if there is some kind of restriction against what this developer wants to do."

"Or maybe we could lobby against it somehow," Jenna suggested.

"I hate to remind you," Dillon said sensibly, "but that camp is in an unincorporated area of Grundman County. St. Mary's city hall has no jurisdiction over that area."

"Then we'll have to figure out something else," Paul insisted. "That developer has got to be stopped. What he's doing is immoral."

"Why do you say that?"

Megan jumped at the sound of Rick's calm voice. Things were going from bad to worse.

"I beg your pardon?" Paul said, not understanding.

"Why do you think putting up condominiums is immoral?"

Paul fudged a little. "Well, condominiums in themselves are not immoral, I suppose. It just doesn't seem right to destroy the Homestead so some rich guy can make a big profit."

Rick proceeded casually but directly. "So it's immoral because this camp will be lost."

"Yeah," Paul said with his mouth full. "A lot of little people are paying the price for somebody who probably doesn't need those condominiums."

"Like a lot of little people are paying the price so you can indulge in the American tradition of overeating while millions are starving around the world?"

Paul was caught off guard and had no answer. He stopped chewing and looked up at Rick, puzzled.

"I'm your big bad corporate developer," Rick explained. "Actually, there's no big corporation, there's just me, trying to make the best use of the opportunity before me and use my gifts to create something of beauty and value. I don't see how that is any more immoral than intending to eat your way through the next six weeks like a glutton."

"I'm sorry," Paul mumbled, "I didn't know. . ."

"There are a lot of things you people don't know," Rick went on. "It's not like I'm trying to put a toxic waste center in your backyard or a gambling casino in the middle of the elementary school. I'm talking about building homes to accommodate the growth that will inevitably come to Grundman County in the next few years."

"But that camp is valuable, too," Donna insisted. "What right do you have to barge in and do away with something people around here care about?"

"The fact is that the owner of the property intends to sell it. If he doesn't sell it to me for condominiums, he'll sell it to someone else." Rick's voice was calm and steady, but he obviously had more to say. Megan's eyes settled on her plate as she listened to him.

"Please excuse my brashness," Rick went on, "but you've been quite judgmental without accurate information. I fail to see how that attitude is any less destructive of decent values than what you are accusing me of doing."

Megan wanted to crawl into a hole. How had she ever thought that these two worlds could meet without colliding? Alone with Rick, she somehow managed to make the two views compatible—or at least block out their contradictions. But here, in this room full of people who opposed Rick's project, there was no escaping the fact that eventually she would have to make a choice between loyalty to the camp and enthusiasm for Rick's project.

"I think we all share similar values," Brad said diplomatically. "You're right, Rick, that it is presumptuous of us to think that we have any right to determine what happens to that property. Please forgive us."

"I understand your feelings," Rick said, his jaw set tight and his voice more controlled. "But you have to look at the whole picture."

Stacie asked for the butter and rolls and others attempted to lighten the conversation again. But the damage was done. A heavy cloud hung over the room, and no one dared to say anything substantial.

"If you'll excuse me," Rick said finally, "my sister agreed to let me come here only on condition that I also spend part of the day with her family." He squeezed Megan's hand under the table. "Why don't you come over when you're ready, Megan?" he suggested. "I'll see you over there later."

eight

December arrived with a wintry blast that eradicated any sense of autumn. Soon after Thanksgiving, the daytime temperature dipped into the low twenties and settled there. Fierce icy winds ripped through the region around St. Mary's.

Undaunted by these conditions, the citizens welcomed the holidays. Christmas lights soon illuminated the eaves of most of the houses, and Santa was seen on lawns all over town. *Less frequently,* Megan thought, *someone quietly set out a nativity scene as a quiet reminder of the true season.*

Megan would have preferred to spend Saturday in her fire-warmed apartment, but Rick had pleaded with her to visit the Homestead with him. Stanton W. Phillips wanted to meet Rick on the property to discuss the terms of their deal.

"But it's freezing out there!" Megan had protested that morning when Rick called and asked her to come along.

"I'll find a way to keep you warm," he promised. "I don't want to spend the whole day away from you."

"Well..." More than the cold weather kept Megan from agreeing enthusiastically. The conflict of Thanksgiving dinner raged unresolved inside her; going to the camp and meeting Stanton Phillips would certainly aggravate her torment. But there was some consolation in the thought of being with Rick, so in the end she gave in and bundled up against the bitter cold air.

Now Megan stood on the front step of the cottage where

Margaret Barrows's belongings were still stacked in cardboard boxes. With her hands in her pockets and a scarf tied around her neck, she took a deep breath and tried to relax. When she exhaled, her warm breath hung in the air as if it might stay there and freeze in place. Her back already ached from her body's involuntary stiffening against the cold.

Rick nervously paced around the immediate vicinity, anxious to explore the property but hesitant to be anywhere except at the entrance when Phillips arrived. His whole future was riding on this business opportunity. So far he had dealt with Stanton Phillips's lawyer, usually through his own lawyer. He had admitted to Megan that he was intimidated by a personal meeting with someone whose decision could determine his future.

The moment Megan had been dreading all day arrived. Stanton Phillips had spared no expense in renting a car at the airport fifty miles away to deliver him in style to the rural property which he owned. The sleek black stretch limousine could barely negotiate the curves in the narrow road leading to the camp.

The dirt road, which the county refused to pave because it was used so little, was not meant for a luxury automobile. Megan winced as she saw the rear axle dip low into a neglected rut. Slowly, the driver pulled the vehicle around the circular drive and parked in front of the cottage. Megan followed silently as Rick took her by the hand and led her to the side of the limousine. The driver got out and ceremonially opened the rear door for his employer.

Stanton Phillips unfolded his lanky frame and emerged from the car. Megan judged that he was in his early forties and trying too hard to be younger. His black hair, expensively cut, was longish in the back and dropped over the collar of his imported ski jacket. Around his neck he sported a bright red scarf, the only relief to an otherwise imposing image.

"I'm glad you could make it, Avery," Phillips said, dispensing with introductions. "Let's have a look around, shall we?" Then he seemed to notice that Rick was not alone. He raised one eyebrow and awaited an explanation for Megan's presence.

"This is Megan Browning," Rick said, "a good friend of mine. Actually she knew your aunt quite well."

"Is that so?" asked Phillips.

"Only recently," Megan clarified. "I was part of the group that helped get the camp cleaned up last spring when Margaret wanted to get it running again."

"I see." Phillips showed no emotion, either about the camp or his aunt.

Megan did not want to be there—and she was already shivering—but she was determined to be cooperative and pleasant for Rick's sake. "I admired your aunt very much," she offered. "Were you able to see her often?"

He shook his head. "I haven't been here for twenty years. I meant to come to the funeral, but some last minute business kept me in California." He glanced around with a half-smirk on his face. "From what I see so far, the place hasn't changed much."

Megan was not sure how to take that statement. She supposed it was true enough, but derision in his tone was obvious. She decided not to reply. She liked him less in person than she had by reputation.

"Well, perhaps we should get started," Rick said. "If we walk quickly enough, we may even stay warm." His eyes flickered at Megan and he gave her a forced smile.

They started up the hill leading to the cabins. Megan trailed behind the men a few steps. Every few minutes Rick would glance back over his shoulder at her, but she made no move to walk alongside him. Stan Phillips was the leader of this expedition, and she was less and less sure she wanted to be part of it.

Stan reached into his pocket and pulled out a pack of cigarettes. Unencumbered by his snugly fitting gloves, he lit a cigarette with the quick skill of long habit. He inhaled deeply and seemed to hold his breath a long time before exhaling. Megan watched passively as the smoke rose into the cold air, glad that she was not any closer to him.

They reached the first set of cabins. "As I understand it, Avery," Stan said, "this is where you propose to put the main set of buildings."

"Yes, here at the top of the hill," Rick explained, stopping and gesturing around. "The tennis courts would be down below in that direction, and beyond that the other units."

Stan threw down his half-smoked cigarette and snubbed it out with his right foot. "I always hated this place."

"I beg your pardon?" Rick said.

"I always hated coming here. For six years, my parents made me come here to spend the summer while they went off to Europe."

"They probably thought Europe would not be very interesting for a little boy," Rick said. Megan could see he was fumbling for something to say. "Every kid dreams of going to summer camp."

"Yeah, well, I hated it. Every year."

"I'm sure your aunt and uncle enjoyed seeing you," Megan instinctively tried to come to Rick's rescue.

Stanton Phillips raised her eyes at her comment, and immediately she was sorry she had spoken.

"They were all right, except a little too religious as I look back on it now. But I was a California kid. They had no business making me spend my summers here."

Rick and Megan stole a glance at each other. Obviously this topic of conversation would lead nowhere.

"If you buy the land, it's up to you what you do with it," Stan said. "But I think you could build a lot more on these acres than you have planned."

"I'd like to retain some of the serene setting," Rick explained. "I think it will increase appeal to the buyers of the units."

"You could increase your profit considerably by putting the first complex closer to the road and duplicating it on the other side of the property, instead of doing a smaller complex over there."

Rick responded cautiously. "I appreciate your advice. Perhaps I'll reconsider and leave room to expand later."

"When do you plan to start construction?"

Megan pretended to be interested in the scenery and looked away as she listened for Rick's answer.

"I've had the plans drawn for some time now," he said. "I've just been looking for the right piece of land. So the next hurdle would be getting these structures cleared away."

Stan Phillips laughed coarsely. "Well, if you blow hard enough, they'll come tumbling down, I'm sure. That shouldn't hold you up too long."

Megan had reached her limit with Stan Phillips and his snobbery. "Rick," she said, "I'll think I'll go back to the cottage and wait for you there. I'm sure you and Mr. Phillips have plenty to talk about."

"Are you sure?"

"Yes. I'm getting cold, actually. Take your time. I'll see you later."

She did not give Rick a chance to change her mind. Immediately, she turned around and started back down the hill toward the stone cottage.

Deep in her pocket, her hand was wrapped around the key that would let her into the welcome warmth of a place Stan Phillips obviously detested. As quickly as she could, she pushed open the door and stepped into the maze of boxes, grateful for any physical barrier she could possibly put between herself and Stanton W. Phillips.

Alone in the cottage, Megan stared out the front window. There was no heat, but at least she was out of the wind—and away from Stanton Phillips. She would have liked something hot to drink, but everything in the kitchen, including the copper teakettle, had already been sorted through and packed away. There was hardly any place to sit down amid all the boxes.

So she stood and stared out the window. The black limousine, its engine still running for warmth, was an irritating intrusion on a familiar scene. Megan had to remind herself that the limo driver was an innocent character in this ridiculous plot; he had simply been hired to drive a car and had done his job.

Megan was cold. She was ready to go back to town. It seemed like a long time before Rick and Stan returned to view. She was expecting Phillips to get in his limo, but instead he came to the door with Rick. She opened it and let them in.

"Mr. Avery tells me that you have kindly packed up the contents of the house," he said politely but stiffly. "I will leave instructions with my lawyer about getting rid of everything."

"There are some photos and things you might want," Megan said. "Family pictures, I think." *Couldn't he call it something besides 'getting rid of everything'?* Megan wondered.

Phillips shook his head. "I'm not interested in a trip

down memory lane. Thank you for getting things boxed up. You don't need to concern yourself with my aunt's belongings any further."

He offered his hand to Rick. "I think we have come to an agreement, Avery. My lawyer will be in touch with you."

Rick smiled, obviously pleased with the deal they had struck. "I'll be waiting."

Megan felt a sick sensation in her stomach. Rick was really going through with this; she could deny it no longer. While Rick walked with Stanton out to the waiting limo, a tear escaped her eye and dribbled down one cheek. Something quietly snapped inside her.

Rick quickly returned to the cottage. "Ready to head back?" he asked. "I'll get the car warmed up." Then he noticed her tearing eyes. "What's wrong, Megan? Don't you feel well?"

"You know what's wrong, Rick," she said. "I should never have let you talk me into coming out here today. You really want to tear down this camp and build a place nobody in St. Mary's could afford to live in."

"Megan, honey, it's a business deal."

"You promised me you would reconsider. You know what this camp means to me and a lot of other people."

"I promised I would reconsider; I didn't promise to change my mind," Rick said defensively. "Believe me, I thought about your feelings. But Stanton Phillips is determined to sell this property. You saw for yourself how much he hates this place. If he doesn't sell it to me, he'll sell it to someone else, and the camp will still be lost."

"How can you stand to do business with a man like that?" Megan flashed.

"Because it's just business, Megan. I'm not going to live with him. I've got a good lawyer looking out for me, and I really think this is a good deal."

"I didn't like him at all, Rick."

"It doesn't really matter if we like him. Once the deal is closed, we don't ever have to see him again."

Rick crossed the room and came and stood behind Megan. He wrapped his arms around her and leaned his chin on her shoulder. "Megan, please try to understand. I've waited a long time for a chance like this. I've been praying for it for years. This deal is just too good to pass up."

Megan was silent and did not return Rick's affectionate embrace.

"Megan, please say something," Rick pleaded.

"I guess we don't know each other as well as I thought we did," she finally said, quietly.

"What do you mean by that?" Rick pulled away and moved around to look at Megan's face.

"I don't think we should keep seeing either other, Rick."

"What! I love you, Megan, don't you believe that?"

"I don't know what to believe. I just know that we want different things, so I don't see how we have a future together."

"Megan, one thing is business and the other is personal. They don't have anything to do with each other."

"I can't separate them, Rick. You want to tear down a camp that I want to see keep going. It's not easy for me to say, 'Oh, well, that's business.'"

Rick sighed. "Megan, let's drive back to town and talk about this somewhere warm, okay?"

"I think it would be better if you just took me home, Rick."

For a long, tortuous moment, Rick was silent and did not move. At last he said, "I'll get the car."

nine

"See you Monday!" Megan waved good-bye to the busload of children and stood for a moment to watch the yellow bus lumber out of the parking lot and turn onto the street. After the usual chaos that comes from spending six hours a day with a bunch of five-year-olds, she was glad it was Friday again.

She could hardly believe there were only two more weeks of school before the Christmas break began. The weeks of the fall semester had flown by—until that week. The last six days had been the longest and most grievous time in her life.

At some moments, she wished she could turn back the clock and avoid meeting Rick Avery in the first place. Then she would shake her head and say to herself, *I would't trade those few weeks for anything.*

Exposed on the sidewalk, she began to feel the cold. Megan hugged her coat close against the icy wind and scurried through the front door into the welcome warmth of the school building. As she walked down the hall to her classroom, she heard only the click of her flat heels against the gray and red tile.

She wanted to get her room cleaned up and head for home as quickly as possible that Friday afternoon. The weather forecaster on the morning news had predicted a six-inch snowfall for Friday evening, and Megan wanted to stop by the grocery store and get home before the weather turned nasty.

On her desk, she found a pink square slip of paper that

had not been there when she left the room earlier. It was a phone message. *Please call Rick*, said the polite hand-writing of the school secretary. *Important*.

Dispirited, Megan drooped into the chair behind her desk. Rick had phoned her every night that week, and every time she had let the message machine pick up the call. Now he was calling at work, too.

She had been silent during the ride home from the camp on the previous Saturday—and grateful that Rick had not pressed her. But she had resisted his attempts to hold her or kiss her when they had reached her apartment, and she had not asked him to come in. Although her last words at the camp had surprised even her, she meant them.

She had skipped church on Sunday because she thought he might be there and had allowed herself to fall into a despondent funk. If only he would not torture her with the sound of his smooth, gentle voice on the answering machine every night, then she might be able to get back to normal.

Megan simply could not bring herself to want what Rick wanted—to tear down the camp. And obviously he did not want what she wanted—to keep it going. Logically, she understood that if Rick did not buy the land, Stanton Phillips would sell it to someone else and the camp would still be lost. In one sense, what Rick was doing was quite reasonable and a good business move. Still, Megan hated the thought of being connected to the transaction.

Most of all, she wished that somehow Rick could care about the camp. To Megan, the camp was more than just a piece of land up for grabs because of the death of its owner. Despite what Rick said, she believed the land offered more than simply a wise business opportunity.

Enfolded in a romance sweeter than she had ever known, Megan had put aside the conflict for as long as she could.

But she had reached her limit. The day had come when reality intruded on the web that handsome Rick was spinning around her, and she no longer believed that it was possible to be wrapped up in Rick without feeling the loss that his success would mean. She could not share his success, and he would never understand her loss.

Everyone thought Megan was so sensible and level-headed, but she certainly did not feel that way when she was around Rick. Maybe it was not possible to be her true self when she was with him, and eventually she would wonder what had happened to the person she thought she was.

On the other hand, maybe she felt different with Rick because he somehow brought out her true self, and now that she had broken up with him, she would never discover the person she might be.

Megan shook her head and crumpled the pink telephone message in one fist. No, she would not call Rick back. She would stick with the level-headed Megan that she knew best.

Her sensible head told her lovesick heart that she had only known Rick for a few weeks and it would be better to break things off early. Hearing his gentle voice on the answering machine each day was difficult.

Twice she had reached for the phone to call him back and tell him to forget everything she had said last Saturday. But she had not done it. She was convinced that they were simply too different from each other; someday the passion would wear off, and they would find they had nothing else in common.

In the stillness of her empty classroom, Megan could hear the clock ticking—a sound she never heard when the children were there. A low hum in the background told her that the baseboard heater was running in a steady battle against the frosty air pressing against the windows.

Somehow these small signals of ordinary life were comforting. Even though Stacie thought Megan was a romantic, maybe her life was simply not meant to be exciting.

Hearing a rush of wind, Megan looked up and then glanced out the window at the darkening sky. Remembering the threat of bad weather, she started moving again. The children had done a fairly good job of putting things away, so there was not much to do.

She could take home the stack of forms to start preparing for parent-teacher conferences right after New Year's. Hastily, she pushed the folder into her tote bag and reached for her black lesson planning book as well. She could easily spend the whole weekend working.

She had just buttoned the last button on her coat and flipped her scarf around her neck when her principal entered the room.

"Hi, Megan. I'm glad you're still here."

Megan forced herself to brighten her mood. "Hi, Carol. What can I do for you?"

"Actually this is a personal visit," Carol said, and Megan's stomach did a nervous flip. "Rick has been moping around my house all week. I've never seen him so depressed. He won't tell me anything except that you don't want to see him anymore."

Megan turned her face toward the window. "That's right. I think it will be better this way."

Carol did not speak for a moment. "Megan, I admit my first instinct is to share my brother's feelings. I want him to be happy. But I care about you, too, after three years of working together."

"I appreciate that, Carol," Megan said, turning to face her boss again. "I don't want you to get caught in the middle of this."

"And I don't want to stick my nose in where it doesn't belong," Carol was quick to add. "But if there is something I can do. . ."

Megan shook her head. "No, there's nothing you can do, but thank you for caring. Just give Rick some time. We were only seeing each other for a few weeks, after all. He'll be fine."

"And what about you?" Carol asked softly.

Megan swallowed the wave of emotion that surged up inside her. She was a hair's breadth away from rushing into arms that she knew were ready to welcome her. But she said only, "I'll be fine, too, with some time."

Carol pressed her lips together and nodded wordlessly. When she spoke, she changed the subject. "It's getting dark. We'd both better get out of here before the snow starts." With a fleeting smile, she left Megan alone again.

Outside once more, Megan thought the temperature had dropped ten degrees in the last thirty minutes. She pulled the hood of her coat up over her head and tightened the scarf around her neck. The sky, already its usual late afternoon gray color, seemed particularly bleak. As she navigated across the parking lot to her car, she had to watch for patches of ice that were hard to see in the dimness.

Not until she reached her car did she look up and see that Rick was standing next to it. It was too late to pretend she hadn't seen him.

"Hello, Rick," she said, fumbling with her car keys. *How long has he been standing there?* she wondered. *Was he there when I put the kids on the bus and I just didn't notice?*

"Megan, I've been calling you all week." His tone held no note of chastisement. His voice was as smooth and natural as the messages he had been leaving every night.

"I know." She avoided looking at his eyes.

"Can't we please talk? Let me take you somewhere for some coffee or hot chocolate."

"I really just want to get home before the storm starts." She jiggled her keys again, but Rick was leaning against the door.

"I know you don't like what's happening to the camp land," Rick said, "but it's not my fault that Phillips doesn't want to run a kids' camp." Now he was starting to sound frustrated, and Megan began to feel alarmed.

"I didn't say it was your fault," she said softly.

"Then why don't you want to see me anymore? Why are you avoiding me?"

"We're too different, Rick. We want different things. I just think it'll be easier if we break up now. It would be so much harder later." She nearly lost control of her voice.

"Why are you so sure we would break up later?" he challenged.

"Please, Rick," she said, "it's cold out here. Just let me go home."

"I think you owe me more of an explanation, Megan," he insisted. "It's like someone pushed a button in you last Saturday, and suddenly I'm out of the picture. There was no warning, nothing I could do to defend myself."

"You don't have to defend yourself, Rick. You haven't done anything wrong."

Rick cocked his head and listened for more.

"I suppose that doesn't make any sense to you," Megan said. "But it was just too hard for me. We don't want the same things, Rick. Last Saturday made that clear to me. I couldn't avoid it any longer."

"One thing is business, the other personal. They don't have anything to do with each other."

"You want me to separate business from our personal

relationship," she said. "I'm not sure I can do that."

"Have you even tried?" he said, accusingly.

She had no response. She heard a sharpness in his voice that she had never heard before. That only reminded her that she really did not know him very well.

"Fine, Megan," he finally said, stepping aside. "It's too cold to stand out here and argue with you. Have it your way."

Rick walked away without looking back. Shivering, Megan unlocked her car and got in. She turned the key in the ignition and waited for the engine to warm up. Involuntarily, her eyes followed the fading figure of Rick as he crossed the lot to where his own car was parked. He literally disappeared into the gray sky behind him.

Megan choked on the knot in her throat. What had she said good-bye to?

ten

Megan snapped the lid on the small container and put the rest of the stew back in the refrigerator. The biscuit she had warmed up was now cold and unappetizing and so stale that she was sure she would never eat it. She tossed it in the trash.

For the fourth night in a row, Megan had tried to eat a decent dinner and failed. On the weekend, while it snowed steadily outside, she had tried to perk herself up by cooking a large pot of beef and vegetable stew and baking powder biscuits from scratch.

The mingled aromas deliciously filled the apartment as the stew simmered most of the day on Saturday, and Megan had enjoyed that. But when it came time to actually eat, even five hours of anticipation did not revive her appetite. In the end, she had put most of the stew in the freezer and kept only a little of it out. She had been picking at that portion for three days now, never managing to eat much of it.

"Well, Franklin," Megan said aloud, "It's Tuesday, and I promised Stacie I would help with the wedding invitations." She bent over and scooped up the cat and laid her cheek against his soft fur. "I'm not really in the mood for stuff like that, but I did promise, so I guess I'd better go."

Franklin squirmed out of her arms.

"Oh, come on! Are you going to pout because I'm going out? Give me a break. Except to go to work, I haven't been out of the apartment for a week and a half."

Unimpressed by Megan's defense, Franklin slinked off to the living room to find his favorite couch cushion. Megan scowled at him. She felt no guilt about going out. Franklin had had plenty of attention in the last few days.

Without Rick around to invite her out, she had quickly returned to her familiar homebody existence. She had done some Christmas shopping, but for the most part she thought it was too much effort to fight the weather and roads to get out. So she stayed home in the evenings and even all through the weekend. For the second Sunday in a row, she had skipped church.

When Stacie called, pleading for help with her wedding invitations, Megan suspected it was just a ploy to get her out of the apartment, but she agreed. The truth was that she was starting to feel closed in, so even if Stacie's invitation was a pretense, Megan knew it would do her good to get out for the evening.

Megan set her plate in the sink and went into the bedroom. She pulled off her skirt and blouse and replaced it with her heaviest jeans and a thick sweatshirt with a turtleneck underneath. If she had to face the winter night air, she was going to be prepared for it. A glance in the mirror told her that her pony tail needed to be tidied, but she just smirked at her image and left her hair as it was, straggly and frizzy. *It's just Stacie,* she told herself.

In the living room she pulled her ski jacket out of the closet and hung up the gray coat she had worn to school. Franklin was snoozing on the couch.

"I don't suppose you care, but I'm leaving now," Megan said, and she went out the door with a mixture of reluctance and relief.

"Can you hand me that roll of stamps?"

Megan numbly pushed the stamps to within Stacie's

reach and mechanically straightened the stack of wedding invitations they had finished.

"I lost my list!" Stacie said suddenly, shuffling papers around on her dining room table. "It was here just a minute ago."

Megan joined in the search and realized her elbow was firmly planted on Stacie's missing list. "Here it is," she said, pulling it out from under her arm. "How many more of these do you have to do, anyway?"

"About sixty, I think."

"It sounds like this wedding is going to be bigger than I thought."

Stacie shook her head. "Not really. I don't expect most of the out-of-town people will come. But Brad's mother sent a list of every distant relative he has, and she wants them all to get invitations."

"And how is your mother-in-law to be?" Megan asked.

Stacie gave a short laugh. "She's in a state of near-panic. She's convinced something is going to go wrong—like nobody will come to the wedding because I waited so long to send out the invitations."

Megan smiled at the thought of a formal wedding party and an empty church.

"Actually," Stacie continued, "she's been great about everything. I haven't heard from my father since the day he left us, and since my mother died, I haven't really felt like I had a family. Now I'm going to be part of one again."

"I hope you're ready for that brood!" Megan cautioned.

She reached for a stack of envelopes with addresses on them and resumed her task: first placing the pale blue card in an inner envelope and then sliding that into the larger outer envelope. She picked up a reply card and slid it in as well. Then she turned it over and read the name on the outside.

"Owen Jamieson!" Megan exploded with laughter. "I haven't thought about him in ages. Are you still in touch with him?"

Stacie smiled deviously. "Only now and then."

"What exactly does that mean?"

"Oh, Christmas, birthdays, that sort of thing."

"What does Brad think about your inviting an old flame to your wedding?"

Stacie shrugged. "He wasn't really a flame. More like a flicker. Besides, I heard he got engaged recently."

"Not to Steffie Murdock, I hope," Megan said, starting to giggle.

Stacie giggled, too. "Steffie Murdock. Now there's someone I haven't thought about since graduation day."

"You mean she's not on your invitation list?" Megan feigned shock.

"Are you kidding! Then something *would* go wrong with the wedding."

"I can understand. She's the sort anyone would want to block out of their memory."

"I never understood what Owen saw in her. He seemed so sensible."

"Obviously he was on the rebound," Megan said with an air of authority, "after you dumped him for Brad."

"Oh, get out of here," Stacie retorted. "There was nothing to dump." She slid another stack of envelopes across the table toward Megan. "Stop harassing me and get back to work."

For a while they did not speak. But the memory of Owen Jamieson and Steffie Murdock stirred up thoughts of other college friends for Megan, of dates that did not go quite right and relationships that ended sooner than she had hoped, of long weekend evenings alone in the library while the other girls—even Steffie—had had dates. Her mood changed abruptly.

"Weddings are sure complicated," Megan muttered. "Look at all this stuff. Two envelopes plus a reply card and this silly piece of tissue paper to protect the embossed printing. What does all this have to do with marriage, anyway?"

Stacie was quiet. Megan could feel her friend's eyes on her, even though her hand continued moving the pen across the envelopes in front of her.

"I guess I sound pretty grouchy, huh?"

"Just a little," Stacie agreed.

"Sorry."

"You're entitled." Stacie paused and put her hand on Megan's arm. "Look, if you're not in the mood for this, I understand. I can get Brad to help later tonight."

Megan sighed. "It's all right." She slid an invitation into its envelope. "I don't mean to sound critical of your invitations. I like them a lot, actually."

"You were there when we picked them out. You're the one who found them in the first place."

Megan smiled, remembering. "I was so caught up in your romance. I probably acted like I was the one getting married."

"It was pretty funny, I have to admit," Stacie chuckled. "But you always believed Brad and I would end up together with a storybook happy ending."

"So far I've been right—at least about you." Megan licked a stamp and stuck it on the corner of the envelope. "A month from now you'll be married and living happily ever after. I'll still be eating supper with my cat every night. Franklin and I are both getting fat."

"You're not fat, Megan! " Stacie chastised. "As for Franklin, well, let's just say he could use a little more exercise." She paused. "You're pretty miserable without

Rick, aren't you?" It was more a statement than a question.

"No happy ending for me, I'm afraid."

"Megan, if I knew some magic words to help you, I would say them."

"Thanks, Stace, but I don't know what those words would be."

Stacie put her pen down. "How about some tea?" she said. "Or would you rather have coffee?"

"Tea would be fine." Megan agreed, "but it's not necessary to pamper me."

"I'm not," Stacie said. "I need a shot of caffeine if I'm going to get this job done tonight. I can't believe I waited this long to do it."

"Why isn't Brad helping?" Megan asked, following Stacie into the kitchen. "After all, they're his relatives."

"Because I foolishly told him I wanted to do it myself." Stacie filled the kettle and set it on the stove. "Talk about an unrealistic romantic notion! Maybe you're right; maybe all this fuss and bother about the wedding is too much." She stretched her arms above her head wearily. "I'll be worn out by the time it gets here."

"It'll be a perfect wedding. And you wouldn't have it any other way." Megan took down a couple of mugs and set a tea bag in each one. "You'll always be happy with Brad." She choked on her last sentence.

"Megan, you'll be happy, too. Maybe not with Rick, but with someone else."

"I'm not so sure, " Megan said softly.

"You made a good decision, Megan," Stacie said. "Rick seemed nice enough, but you said yourself that you didn't really have much in common with him. That probably would have made things harder in the longer run."

"If it was a good decision, why am I so miserable?"

Megan wanted to know. "Why do I feel so lost?"

"Maybe you just got caught up in the romance of it all," Stacie offered.

Megan vehemently shook her head. "No, that wasn't it. Rick was not just a fairy tale. He was the real thing."

Stacie filled the mugs with steaming water and, with one in each hand, led the way back to the other room. "Well, I didn't really have a chance to get to know him. But I know you, and you have good reasons for the things you do. I trust your judgment completely. I'm sure it's for the best that you broke up."

"That's easy for you to say," Megan shot back with an uncharacteristic edge to her voice.

"What do you mean?" The tone had not gone unnoticed by Stacie.

"You have Brad. You're getting married in a few weeks. Everything is working out for the best for you."

Stacie set her mug down solidly on the table. "Megan, listen to yourself," she said. "I'm trying to support you. I didn't tell you to break up with Rick. You decided that by yourself."

"You're pretty quick to agree with it, though," Megan said.

"If you don't think it's for the best, why did you do it?"

Megan slumped in her chair and put her head down on her arm. "I don't know. I don't know what's for the best. I want Rick. I love him. But I just don't think I fit into his life."

Stacie stopped talking long enough to sip some tea. "Missed you at church on Sunday," she said. "The last two Sundays, actually."

"I know," Megan said reticently. "I just wasn't up to it. I haven't been myself."

"Rick hasn't been there either."

Megan busied her fingers with the handle of her mug and didn't say anything. Stacie always could read her mind. Obviously, she knew Megan was afraid of running into Rick at church.

"This is not the first time you've broken up with someone," Stacie reminded her. "Remember Steve Jackson? And Nathan Howard? You really thought you were going to marry Nathan Howard."

Megan lifted her head. "But now I know the difference, Stacie. What I felt for Nathan is nothing like what I feel for Rick. I remember the day you came back to the dorm after meeting Brad."

"You couldn't stop giggling at me when I told you about him."

"You had been transported to another planet, and I found it very amusing." Megan spoke quietly. "But now I understand. I know why you felt the way you did."

Stacie sipped her tea in silent understanding.

Megan continued. "And now I understand how you felt when you thought you couldn't marry Brad after he broke your engagement." Her shoulders twitched in a sob. "I don't want to feel this way, Stace. I want a happy ending, too."

eleven

Rick stopped calling.

Megan sat alone in her apartment for the next several evenings, stroking Franklin's back and rummaging through the dog-eared paperback novels stacked around the living room. Occasionally she would turn on the television and find solace in the sound of a human voice other than her own. Once when the phone rang, her heart leaped to her throat, but it was only a recorded sales pitch for aluminum siding that she did not need.

There were no more messages on her answering machine, no more pink slips of paper from the school secretary. Her principal did not mention her brother again, although seeing Carol always made Megan think about Rick even more.

On one level, Megan was relieved at the silence. After all, it was what she had said she wanted; finally, he was respecting her wishes. At the same time, her heart sank deeper into despondency at the thought that Rick had given up without more of a fight. When he was calling her every day, she still felt like he wanted her. Now she was left only with her desire for him and the reality that he was out of reach.

Megan had a long list of Christmas gifts not yet purchased and a stack of Christmas cards that needed her signature and a personal note. She worked intermittently at these holiday tasks, not relishing them as she usually did. White snow nearly eight inches deep blanketed the land, and the roads were constantly icing over. She had less and less enthusiasm for the Christmas crowds and was beginning to wish she had taken advantage of the batch of mail order catalogues that had been stuffed in her mailbox a few weeks earlier.

Despite her lack of enthusiasm, she was grateful for the tasks that demanded her attention. The challenge of being ready for Christmas day was always before her. A thorough list of things to do kept her moving one foot in front of the other when she might have stayed in bed for three days in a row.

It was time to get a Christmas tree, she decided. Surely that would put her in a holiday mood. While she was growing up, her family always waited until Christmas Eve to go out and cut the perfect Christmas tree and stay up late decorating it. Even as a child, though, Megan begged to have the tree earlier. Now she could do as she pleased, and she usually put one up by the middle of the month.

Christmas music would be a great help, too. In a burst of energy, she foraged through her box of cassette tapes and filled her apartment with strains of English choirs singing carols.

The week passed routinely, and Megan convinced herself that she felt better with each day. It had done her good to get out Tuesday evening. She was less inclined to mope around the apartment, mourning what she could not have. She was more interested in pursuing the pleasure within her reach.

When the week cycled around to Saturday once again, Megan headed over to Stacie's apartment to deliver a silk flower centerpiece she had arranged for the head table at Stacie and Brad's wedding reception. With the bulky box awkwardly lodged in her arms, she twisted around and leaned on the doorbell with one elbow. Fortunately the door opened almost immediately.

"Oh, Megan, it's gorgeous!" Stacie exclaimed at the

sight of the flowers.

"I can still move things around," Megan said, releasing the box into Stacie's waiting hands.

"No, it's perfect just the way it is."

"I didn't know you did flower arranging," said a male voice. Megan looked up to see Dillon Graves coming around the corner from the kitchen. "I thought your specialty was paper dolls and snowflakes."

Megan chuckled. "Hi, Dillon. I didn't know you were here."

"We have to work today," lamented Stacie. "I have a pile of paperwork to get done before I can go on my honeymoon."

"How much did you pay Dillon to get him to help you?" Megan asked playfully.

"Too much!" said Stacie.

"Not enough!" said Dillon.

"Besides," Stacie said, ignoring Dillon's interjection, "Brad is off Christmas shopping, and he was adamant that I could not come along." She eyed Megan suspiciously. "Has he been having any secret conversations with you?"

"My lips are sealed."

"As long as you're here, sit down and I'll get you a cup of coffee. We were about to take a break anyway. I've got a new coffee cake recipe I tried out."

"Food? You don't have to ask twice." Megan slipped her yellow ski jacket off and slung it over the back of an armchair. She followed Stacie and Dillon in to the table and sat down. "Is the table still under here somewhere?" she asked, gently nudging a pile of papers.

"Just clear yourself a spot and be quiet," Stacie scolded. She set a plate down in front of Megan. A slice of moist yellow coffee cake with a swirl of something brown and creamy looked very tempting. "Take a bite and tell me what you think."

Megan chewed for a moment. "That's pretty good. You made this?"

"Of course. Don't sound so surprised."

"It tastes like something Margaret Barrows would have made."

"Well, you caught me," Stacie admitted. "I got the recipe from her last summer. I just never got around to trying it out before."

Megan took another bite. "She'd be proud of your effort."

"I remember the coffee cakes she served on opening day of the camp last year," said Dillon, helping himself to another slice. "I didn't realize she had made all those goodies by herself."

"I'd forgotten you were there when the camp opened," Stacie said. "You never did tell me why you came. After all—"

"After all, you had just dumped me." Dillon finished her sentence with a smile. "I was curious, I guess. And I'm glad I was there when you and Brad decided to get engaged again. I could see for myself that he was the right man for you."

"Thanks for understanding."

"No problem. Back to Mrs. Barrows. I've always wondered how she and her husband got started with that camp in the first place."

Megan and Stacie looked at each other with questioning expressions.

"I don't know for sure," Stacie said. "It was so long ago. They were in their forties when they bought the property and started clearing it."

"But it's a pretty ambitious thing to decide to open a camp for kids," Dillon persisted.

Megan shrugged as she chewed. "They loved kids and

never had any of their own. You should have seen the photos on the walls of the cottage."

"I can understand that motivation, " Dillon said. "I mean, I don't have kids either, but my heart goes out to the ones who have to come to shelters with their parents."

"I agree," said Stacie. "That's why I was really looking forward to being able to take kids out to the Homestead next summer. But I guess I'd better put that out of my mind."

"Not necessarily," Dillon said. "I have a plan."

"What do you mean?" asked Stacie and Megan together.

"I have an idea I'd like to run past the two of you."

Their curiosity piqued, Stacie and Megan both turned to Dillon. He had not really known Mrs. Barrows very well, so the whole conversation had been unexpected, and Megan had started wondering where it was leading.

"I've been doing some investigating into the camp property."

"You?" Stacie asked, incredulous. "What is your interest in the camp?"

"Don't look so shocked. I was a kid once. I know what it's like to go to summer camp."

"What do you mean, 'investigating,'" Megan asked.

"Well, I called the lawyer of that guy, Stanton W. Phillips, who owns the land now."

"And?"

"And I found out what price he's asking for it. I'm thinking of trying to buy it."

Megan's heart started beating faster. "But Phillips already has a buyer—Rick Avery. They've been working on a deal for weeks."

"Yes, but they haven't signed anything," Dillon said. "I know your boyfriend has been talking to Phillips—"

Megan interrupted. "He's not my boyfriend."

"Oh. You were here together for Thanksgiving. I

assumed. . . Well, anyway, they haven't really settled on a price. I don't know what Avery is offering, but I may make a bid."

Megan and Stacie were stunned. They looked at each other and then back at Dillon.

"Can we assume," asked Stacie deliberately, as if she did not believe what she was hearing, "that if you should buy the property, the camp would keep going?"

Dillon nodded. "You guys have won me over. There's no other place in the county like that camp."

"But it's a lot of money," said Megan quite sensibly. "Rick Avery has several other people who want to invest in his project. Maybe it's none of my business, but I can't help wondering how you could afford something like this."

Dillon shrugged. "I can't. But it wouldn't be the first time I had to do some fund raising."

"Even if you buy the property, who would run the camp? Stacie asked.

Megan's mind was racing. "It would be a huge commitment for someone to take on."

Dillon was nodding at their comments. "I'm going into this with my eyes open," he said. "We have to face reality. Some of those outbuildings are not going to last much longer, and there are major wiring problems in some of the cabins. I know your group worked really hard last spring, but there is a lot more that needs to be done if the Homestead is going to stay in business."

"So we'll work hard again this spring," Stacie said, determined. "I'm sure we can find plenty of people willing to help."

"We may have to tear down some cabins and start all over again," Dillon warned. "There might be some major changes."

"But nothing as major as a condominium complex!" Stacie retorted. "It would still be the same camp."

"Dillon, I'm in shock," Megan said. "Are you sure you want to do this?"

"I can't make any promises," he said soberly. "I don't have a lot of money of my own, so I'll have to be pretty persuasive with people who can afford to take this risk."

"Do you really think Stanton Phillips would consider an offer from you?" Megan asked. "I mean, I was out there with him and Rick a couple weeks ago. It looked to me like they came to an agreement."

"Well, as of the close of business yesterday, they have nothing in writing. I don't know what Phillips told your friend, but according to his lawyer, the bidding process is open until December 31. It can't hurt to let Phillips know he has another interested party."

Without responding, Megan stood up and gathered the plates and coffee mugs to take to the kitchen. Stacie stopped her.

"Megan, what's wrong?"

"Nothing. I'm just clearing the table."

"Don't give me that baloney. You never clear a table unless you have to. Something's bothering you."

Megan sat back down in her chair. "This all seems kind of underhanded to me."

"What do you mean? It's the only glimmer of hope we've had for saving the camp!"

"But it doesn't seem fair to Rick. He's had an understanding with Stanton Phillips for weeks now. How can we come in and just pull the rug out from under him?"

"How can we pass up a chance to save the camp?" Stacie challenged.

"Let's just take one problem at a time," Dillon said. "Megan may be right; perhaps Stanton Phillips won't want to discuss any other offers, despite what the lawyer said. And if he does, I'm not positive I can raise the money we would need."

"I think our chances are good," Stacie said, riding high on the optimism of Dillon's announcement. "From what we know about Phillips, he is interested in getting rid of the property and making a profit. It won't matter to him who the buyer is."

"I'm not so sure," Megan said. "If you had seen him that day at the camp, you'd realize how much he hates that place. No matter what you might offer, Dillon, he might sell it to Rick Avery just because he never liked spending his summers there and wants to wipe out bad memories."

"Well, it can't hurt to explore the possibility," Dillon said cautiously.

"I don't think you have a lot of time," Megan remarked. "My impression was that they were getting very close to settling on the terms of the sale."

Megan could see Dillon was puzzled about why she knew so much about Rick Avery's business when she so quickly denied being involved with him earlier in the conversation. Her face reddened, and she waited through an awkward moment till it became clear that Dillon was not going to press the matter.

Her own dilemma was intensified. Was she really capable of plotting against something that meant so much to Rick? What if this really was the big chance he had been waiting for? It was one thing to stop seeing him and not be involved in the transaction at all. It was another to actively work for a cause that would mean so much disappointment to him. Could she do that?

twelve

Megan was glad she had finally decided to go back to church. She sat contentedly in her usual pew, midway back on the left side. Never in her life had she stayed away from church for purely emotional reasons.

The choir sang one of her favorite Christmas anthems, and the resplendent tree in the front of the sanctuary called her heart back from its straying. Nestled among her fellow worshipers, Megan was right where she belonged.

Looking out the window during the worship service, Megan caught herself thinking it was warmer than it really was. The sky was bright, brighter than it had been for weeks. If the weather held up, perhaps she could take her kindergarten kids out to play in the snow one day. She pictured the small hill behind the school and decided that it would be just about right for five-year-olds to sled down.

In the narthex after the service, Brad snuck up behind her and tickled her ribs.

"Yikes! Don't do that," she scolded.

"Just trying to get your attention."

"Whatever happened to saying good morning?"

Brad sobered up in his comic way. "Good morning, Miss Browning."

"That's better."

"A bunch of us are going sledding. Wanna come?"

"Sure! When?" Her morning musings about the weather had charged her with enthusiasm to be outside.

"Right now. We're gonna run home to change clothes and then meet back here to drive out to Grundman County."

"Grundman County?" Megan had assumed they would sled in St. Mary's.

"Yeah. There's a great hill just across from the Homestead. I've had my eye on it since last summer. It'll be perfect. We can park at the camp and walk across the road."

Megan's mood changed to one of caution. "Are you sure we should do that?"

"We're not going to actually sled on camp property," Brad said. "Besides, the place is empty. No one goes out there. Who would we be bothering?"

"Well. . ."

Brad shrugged his shoulders. "If you decide you want to go, be back here in half an hour."

Megan looked at her watch. "I promised to take a couple junior high girls home. I may not make it back by then. But go without me, and I'll catch up."

"Are you sure?"

"Of course. It won't exactly be the first time I've driven out there alone. I don't want to hold everybody up."

"Okay. See you out there."

The sunny sky was misleading. The temperature was well below freezing as Megan left St. Mary's and drove south into Grundman County. As she had predicted, Megan missed the group's departure by about twenty minutes. Undaunted by her solitude, she set off to join the group in her own car.

Traffic was light on a Sunday afternoon, and the roads were fairly dry despite the snowfall of a few days earlier. The change from the bland gray skies of a few days ago to the glistening sunshine invigorated Megan. She sang aloud as she drove along the highway, feeling more energetic than she had all week.

Once she got out of town and into the rural areas of the county, the white expanse of undisturbed farm fields caught the sun's light and threw it back in her face. But it was cold; even with her heater going full blast, Megan felt the bite of the outside air oozing through the cracks in her car door.

The sledding hill was near the camp, just across the road from the property line. Megan had to slow down considerably when she turned into the dirt road leading to the camp. No snow plow had gone before her; there were only the tracks of packed snow left by earlier traffic.

As soon as she turned off the main road, she felt her tires slip and was immediately alert to the icy condition of the road. For a fraction of a moment, she wondered why they had opted to drive all the way out here to sled when there were several good hills right in town. But she knew those hills would be crowded on a day like this, and the beauty of the remote setting would make their recreation more memorable.

Megan spotted Brad's blue van parked just inside the camp's gate, alongside a couple other vehicles. She glanced across the road and saw Stacie and Donna standing at the top of the hill, poised over a sled. Their bright red and blue ski jackets reflected the glare of the sun almost as much as the white snow around them.

When Megan opened her car door, squealing laughter floated down from the hilltop and hung in the air around her. Inspired and enthused, she unlocked her trunk and pulled out the old wooden sled of her own childhood. The ragged clothesline tied to the front bar had been the reins that steered her to safety many times over the years.

"Megaaaan! Up heeeere!"

Megan looked up to see Stacie waving her up. She returned the wave and energetically started the tedious trek up the hill, towing her sled with one arm. A shiny layer of ice atop the snow crunched under her feet with every step.

Except for the footsteps of the others who had already climbed the hill that afternoon, the hillside had been untouched since the most recent snowfall. The snow was at least eight inches deep, maybe more, and the unfamiliar landscape made it hard to know where the drifts were.

Once, Megan stepped into a hole and her leg sunk into the snow up to her knee. She was glad for her warm, waterproof leggings and high boots. It took her a few minutes to extricate herself from that predicament. She had just started making progress up the hill once more when Brad skidded down the hill toward her.

"Need some help?" he asked.

"A little late, aren't you?" she sassed. "Now that I'm out, you show up."

"I know you like to be independent. I was waiting to be sure I was really needed." Brad took the rope from Megan's hand and pulled the sled behind him. They continued trudging up the hill.

She examined the dusting of snow that covered his clothing. "Looks like you've already been down a few times."

"You won't believe this hill, Megan. It's steeper on the other side than you think, and the snow is really slick today."

"This is the kind of day that makes winter bearable," Megan said. "It's cold, but it's beautiful—the way the ice hangs on the trees like glass and all this pure white color."

"Wait till you see the view from the top of the hill."

Halfway up the hill, Dillon joined them.

"Megan! Glad you got here safe. We were beginning to wonder."

"I wouldn't miss this for anything."

Dillon nodded in agreement. "I can't help wondering if Margaret Barrows ever thought about running winter camps."

"That's a great idea," Megan said enthusiastically. "The hill on the camp property is not as high as this one, but it would do for kids."

"And think of the snowmobiling possibilities," Dillon added.

"I hate to burst your bubble," Brad said, "but I think you're forgetting that the cabins are not heated."

Megan conceded the point. "It would be pretty cold. I have to admit that I'm looking forward to being warm again after I get done playing."

But Dillon was not so easily deterred. "The cabins could be heated. They already have electricity."

"It wouldn't be impossible," Brad agreed, "just a lot of work."

"I think it would be worth it. Running winter weekend camps could be very profitable. It might at least generate enough income to cover the expenses of keeping the place in shape over the winter."

"You sound like you're ready to take over the place," Brad said.

"I wouldn't mind giving it a try," Dillon admitted. "I didn't really know Margaret Barrows, but I think she was a woman of great vision. A little help on the business side could make this place very appealing."

Megan listened as Dillon and Brad compared notes about what could be done to improve the camp facilities and what programs could be introduced to make the most profit from what the facilities could offer. It was a dreamlike conversation for her; she wanted it all to happen, but it was hard to believe that it was possible.

In comparison to Dillon's ideas, the work the group had done last spring was a cosmetic touch-up. Dillon was serious about building a camp that would last for decades.

As she visualized the buildings Dillon described, a shadowy image of Rick Avery darkened her picture. Would it be possible for Dillon to get the property? Did she really want to see Rick hurt in the process?

The trio reached the top of the hill at last. Megan looked back and saw the trail of boot prints and sledding tracks they had left behind them. Her eyes raised to the camp across the road, an innocent postcard picture of seasoned wooden buildings and snow drifts.

"Come on, Megs," called Stacie. "Sit yourself down on that sled of yours and go for a ride."

"That's what I'm here for." Megan roused herself to action. She positioned her sled solidly at the launching point everyone was using and aimed directly down the hillside.

"Why do you keep dragging out that old sled?" Brad taunted. "It's too small for you, and the runners are bent."

"This sled and I go way back," Megan said in defense of her childhood sled. "It has been a faithful friend for twenty years. Why should I abandon it now?"

"Like I said, it's too small for you and the runners are bent," Brad repeated.

"Is that a challenge?"

"Ready when you are," Brad said, snatching up his neon pink sledding disk and positioning it next to Megan's sled.

Stacie laughed but agreed to send them off on the count of three. Brad whizzed by Megan's head almost immediately, and she watched as he leaned one direction and then the other to stay balanced on his circular carrier.

She was not far behind him, though, sitting erect and tugging at the clothesline to steer confidently to safety at the bottom of the hill.

On the way down she passed Jenna, Paul, and Donna trudging uphill with a toboggan behind them. Several others from the church group spotted the hillside with their winter wear and sports gear. A snowball fight broke out between some of the men, and once, Brad maneuvered Megan onto his slick disk and sent her spinning down the hill, unprepared for the thrill of the speed. For more than two hours, they frolicked like small children, uninhibited and carefree.

Exhausted after her sixth trip down the hill and the sixth hike back up the hill, Megan sat on her sled to rest. So far she had managed to keep warm as long as she kept moving, but now she was getting cold.

From her vantage point, she could see that the rest of the group consisted of convenient pairs. Stacie and Brad, Paul and Donna—even Jenna and Dillon seemed to be going down together almost every time.

Suddenly Megan felt out of place. She missed Rick intensely. In only a few short weeks, she had gotten used to the feeling of being part of a pair, and now she was alone again.

"Scoot over." Stacie joined her on the sled and stretched her feet out in front of her.

Megan complied and shifted over a few inches. "Too bad we don't have some hot chocolate up here."

"That would hit the spot," Stacie agreed. "Hey, there's a car down there." She stood up to get a better look down at the road below them. "Someone is waving at us."

Megan stood up and looked. Her mouth dropped in shock. "That's him, Stace."

"Him who?"

"The infamous Stanton W. Phillips," Megan announced.

"I wonder what he wants with us."

"We'll know soon enough. He's coming up."

Gradually the group gathered at the top the hill and waited for Stanton Phillips to ascend the other side.

"Are you people the owners of those vehicles parked on my property?" he called out harshly as soon as he was within earshot.

Brad slid down the hill a few yards to meet him. "Yes, those are our cars."

"I want them off my land."

"Why don't we introduce ourselves." Brad extended his hand. "I'm Brad Davis. If you own the land over there, you must be Mr. Phillips."

"Yes, I am," Phillips said, ignoring Brad's outstretched hand. "I would appreciate it if you would remove your vehicles immediately."

"We didn't realize we would be in anyone's way if we parked there," Brad said. "We just wanted to be off the road. After all, the camp is not in use at this time of year."

"That's not the point. Just move your cars."

"Certainly, we'll move the cars." Dillon was speaking up. "But may I ask what harm we are causing by parking on that corner of your property?"

"You're not causing any harm. I just want you off. It's an insurance risk for anyone to be on the property without permission."

"We're not actually on the property. This hill is part of a public park."

"Your cars are parked illegally." Stanton Phillips was losing patience. "I'm not going to ask you again. Move your cars or I'll call the police." With that, he turned and started back down the hill.

"Guess we'd better call it a day, folks," Brad said.

"It'll be dark soon, anyway," Stacie said, and the others agreed.

They made a plan to meet for hot chocolate at a coffee shop at the edge of St. Mary's and began their descent. They could have taken one last ride down the side of the hill that led to their cars, but the spirit of the day seemed to have dissipated, and they simply dragged their sleds behind them.

They piled into the vehicles and started their engines. Paul and some of the others pulled away, and Brad followed in a few minutes. Megan was at the end of the line. Only when she was about to back out of her parking space did she realize her scarf was missing. With a sigh she looked back at the hill and saw the streak of green near the base.

She could feel the eyes of Stanton Phillips on her as she shut off her engine and got out of the car again. The short walk across the road seemed to take forever under his disapproving scrutiny. Nevertheless, she plodded a few yards up the hill and retrieved her scarf. When she reached her car again, she was as anxious to be gone as he was to see her go.

thirteen

Megan slammed the car door shut, relieved to be on her way at last. She brushed some loose snow off her jacket and pressed her damp bangs back from her eyes. She had enjoyed the day—up until a few minutes ago—but she was looking forward to sitting in a warm and dry restaurant with something hot to drink and her friends gathered around her.

A glance in the rearview mirror showed Stanton Phillips's rented black sedan still parked nearby. Megan assumed he was inside, watching her every move. With a swift motion, she stretched her seat belt over her shoulder and snapped it in place. Then she turned the key in the ignition—but she heard nothing but a tinny click.

Megan's shoulder sagged at the thought of a stalled car in the middle of nowhere with only Stanton Phillips around. She could just picture his hawkish features as he would swoop over her and demand that she move her car even if she had to pick it up and carry it. In her mind's eye, his eyebrows came together in a scowl.

Determined not to be his victim, she pressed the clutch pedal to the floor as tightly as she could. At first there was only an indistinct choking sound, but as she stepped on the gas pedal, the engine caught and idled high and fast.

Stanton Phillips's car had not moved and she had not seen him since he turned his back on the group on the hillside, but Megan felt self-conscious about how long it was taking for her to get going. She backed up toward him and pointed the front end of the car at the gate. The cold engine stalled again as she shifted into drive. "Don't you dare!" Megan said aloud and twisted the key again. Without waiting for the car to warm up, she accelerated and surged through the open gate.

At last she was free of his stare. The magnificent sky of a few hours ago had gotten grayer by the hour. Snow was imminent, so Megan was content to be headed back to town. However, it would have been more satisfying to choose to go home rather than be chased away.

Outside the gate, she stopped on the deserted road to get herself situated. She turned the heat on as high as it would go, although the engine was far too cold to produce any warmth inside the car. With a sigh, she relaxed the tightness in her back that she had not been aware of until that moment and pushed the radio power button.

With her eyes on the road and one hand on the wheel, she turned the tuning knob with the other hand till she found a classical station playing Christmas music. Satisfied, she settled in for the forty-minute drive home. Slowly she pulled out into the road again.

Megan decided to turn on her headlights. With the late afternoon, the sun's brilliance had diminished into a fuzzy grayness. Megan disliked driving at this time of day; she preferred that it be either light or dark.

Suddenly the front end of her car swung sharply to the left. Ice! She had not seen it at all. Gripping the steering wheel with two hands she quickly steered into the spin. It was happening too fast. She took her foot off the gas pedal, furiously hoping that the car would straighten itself out.

It was too late; the rear wheels were off the road. The front of the car rose awkwardly into the air as the back settled deep into the snowdrift that filled an unseen ditch at the side of the road. Even with a seat belt on, Megan's head and shoulder smashed against the door. Instantly she had a massive headache.

The slow, dreamlike sinking motion finally stopped. Stunned, Megan did not move. She was involuntarily staring at the torn ceiling of her car. The engine sputtered and died, the music stopped, and she was left in silence.

Instinctively, she reached for her throbbing head. She gasped at the pain shooting through her shoulder as she moved. Breathing heavily, she slowly lowered her arms and tried to think what to do. Her right leg moved freely, and her right arm was unimpaired. Cautiously, she twisted her neck around, checking for stiffness.

Injuries seemed limited to the side of her body that had slammed into the door. Despite the way her head felt, she did not think she was seriously hurt; but she would need help.

With a wave of panic, Megan realized that Brad and Stacie and the others were probably several miles ahead of her and would not miss her for quite a while. No one else knew where she was. No one except Stanton Phillips, who might have seen the accident. As much as she hated to admit it, Stanton Phillips was her only hope for help.

Blinking several times, Megan realized her vision was fuzzy and her head weighty. She was not at all sure she could withstand the onslaught of pain if she started to move, and she was nearly helpless against a sudden craving for sleep.

I've got to get out of here! her mind cried out. Her limbs refused to move. Her breathing was shallow and quick as she struggled to keep her eyes open and think clearly. *Move, arms! Move!*

With her right arm, she reached across her body and groped for the door handle and pulled on it. Nothing happened. The driver's side of the car was wedged into the snowbank; she would never be able to get the door open.

Gasping, she stretched across the seat for the door handle on the passenger door. With a determined heave and an inward scream, she shoved it upward and opened it as wide as she could. Exhausted from the effort, she fell back into her seat. If she hardly had the strength to open the door, how would she ever be able to climb out?

Again, she reached across the seat, this time pushing her feet against the floor. Immediately, pain shot through her left ankle, and she sat back. The whole left side of her body started to ache. The desperate urge to lie back and close her eyes was nearly irresistible.

Only the cold kept her awake—and sheer fear of what might happen if she lost consciousness out in the cold. Stanton Phillips was the last person in the world she wanted to rely on, but she had no choice. It could be hours before anyone else drove down that isolated road, especially at night.

Gripping the back of the seat with her right arm, Megan inched over the gearshift on the floor between the seats. Once she was in the passenger seat, she paused to rest. Gradually, using the strength in her right arm and back, she pulled herself toward the opening above her.

"Help!" she called out. "Is anybody there?"

No answer.

"Mr. Phillips? Can you hear me?"

Her own voice came back to her on the wind, but she heard no reply.

Energized by her fear, Megan crawled through the open door, wincing with every motion, and steadied herself against the outside of the car. It took every ounce of strength she had to avoid collapsing in the snow.

Carefully twisting her upper body around, she looked back toward the gate to the camp. Somehow she had to get back there. It was starting to snow, and in another few minutes, the gray sky would be black.

Tentatively, Megan tried to stand on her left ankle. She took a few steps and then felt her leg buckle. She gripped the hood of the car and exhaled forcefully as she tried to control the pain. Obviously she would have to hop. Her head felt as if a boulder were rolling around in her head and she leaned back against the hood of the car to steady herself.

Involuntarily, she gave into the urge to lower her face into her hands. How could she possibly hop thirty yards or more when the jarring motion already shot bullets of pain to her head and shoulder? Fear kept her going. She was determined not to pass out alone when she knew Stanton Phillips was just across the road.

Slowly, with short, irregular jerks of her good leg and frequent stops, she made it to the camp entrance. Phillips's car was still parked inside the gate, and she lurched toward it.

"Mr. Phillips! I'm hurt." She knocked on the windshield, but there was no answer. The tinted glass made it difficult to see in. She pressed her face up against the glass and waited for the fuzziness to disappear. A pair of leather driving gloves lay neatly on the dashboard and an area map lay open on the seat, but no one was in the car.

Megan had enough clarity of mind to realize that Stanton Phillips had not driven all the way out there simply to chase trespassers off his property. Apparently he planned to spend some time on the property. At least thirty minutes had passed since she had pulled away in her car; he could be anywhere in the camp.

"Mr. Phillips?" she called again. "It's me, Megan Browning. I need help." She thought she was calling as loudly as she could, but actually she was making very little sound.

Silence.

Frightened, Megan started to sweat inside her jacket and at the same time held her breath against the jabbing daggers of the wind against her face. She turned her frazzled attention to the cottage, the closest building. Perhaps he had gone inside to go through some of his aunt's belongings.

She hobbled toward the cottage, dragging her left foot cautiously through the snow and putting weight on it only when she had to. The front door was ajar; she pushed it open with her fingertips.

"Mr. Phillips?" He must have been there, or the door would be locked. Grateful that it was open, she limped inside. The boxes had all been cleared away, along with most of the furniture. The cottage no longer exuded any of the warmth or presence of Margaret Barrows. But it was shelter from the frigid weather, and Megan welcomed the respite.

Megan remembered the phone in the kitchen. She could call for help! Leaning on the walls and what little furniture was left, she lurched toward the kitchen and threw open the door. The room was oddly vacant, lacking the familiar scent of homemade bread and brewed tea. But the old black dial phone was still there, looking out of place in the deserted kitchen.

Megan picked up the receiver. There was no dial tone. Stubbornly she clicked the buttons in the cradle up and down. "Hello? Hello? Operator?" she pleaded. "Is anyone there?" It was useless. Obviously the phone had been disconnected; she was foolish to think it would still be in service after all these weeks.

She could stand no longer. In a wave of dizziness and panic, she dropped the receiver and slid down the wall.

When she hit the floor, she gasped in pain and blacked out.

fourteen

Megan heard voices and began to stir; two voices, both familiar. Where was she?

Her eyes still closed, Megan turned her head toward the sound. With the motion, an unintended groan passed through her lips.

"Megan! Megan, just lie still."

She swallowed hard and forced her eyes open. The image was gray and fuzzy, but she recognized Rick. He was bent over her, looking into her blurry eyes.

"Rick. How did you. . . Where. . .?" Words that took enormous strength to form were barely audible.

"Shhhh," he said, stroking her cheek with one finger. "Just lie still. Don't talk."

"But. . .how long. . .?"

"We found you about an hour ago. In the kitchen."

"The phone. . ."

"Yes, I know. The phone is not working. Stan had it disconnected last week."

She couldn't keep her eyes open any longer. "Rick. . ."

He pressed her hand between his own. The warmth of his skin flooded her with security. "Megan, just rest. I'm here. I'll take care of you."

She was drifting away again. She could hear the voices murmuring but the words were indistinct. What were they talking about? *Forecast. All night. Ten inches. No help.* The rest was just sounds, background noise to her own struggle for consciousness.

"Rick?"

"I'm right here, baby," he said, squeezing her hand. "I'm not going anywhere."

"My car. I couldn't stop spinning."

"I saw it in the ditch when I got here. It scared the day-lights out of me. I was so relieved to find you."

She tried to shift her position to be able to look at him more directly. Pain sliced through her shoulder, causing her to cry out.

"Tell me what hurts, Megan," Rick said, putting his face close to hers. "How can I make you more comfortable?"

"My head, my shoulder, my ankle," she said hoarsely. "I got thrown against the inside of the door. Everything hurts."

"Your ankle? Which one?"

"The left one."

He put his hand gently on her boot and she flinched.

"We'd better get this boot off, Megan," he said, gently pulling at the top of the boot.

Megan clamped her teeth together and grimaced while Rick worked the boot off an inch at a time. Gently he peeled down her sock to look at her foot. The ankle was swollen and already discolored.

Rick shoot his head. "That doesn't look good. No wonder it hurts."

Megan was starting to take in more of her surroundings. She was in the bedroom, lying on a bare mattress on the floor. Rick was sitting on the edge of it, still holding her hand.

"Most of the furniture is gone," Rick said, seeing the question in her eyes. "The Salvation Army is supposed to come for the bigger things in a few days. Lucky for you, the bed is still here."

She smiled weakly at him. "Lucky for me, you're here. I was looking for Mr. Phillips, trying to get help. I couldn't find him."

"He's here. He was in the shed, out back. I guess he didn't hear you."

"That's right." Stanton Phillips joined the conversation. "I saw you pull out and thought you were on your way with the others. I didn't know anything had happened. As soon as Avery told me he'd seen your car in the ditch, we started looking for you.

Megan lifted herself up on her good elbow. "Thank you. I'm glad you were both here. I think if I'm careful I could move around a little, enough to ride back into town."

Rick and Stanton looked at each other and then back at Megan.

"What's wrong?" she asked.

"It's been snowing heavily for the last two hours," Rick explained. "They were only forecasting a couple inches, but it's turning into a major blizzard."

"I'm afraid we'll have to wait out the storm here," Stan said.

"But the others will be looking for me," Megan protested. "We were going to meet for hot chocolate."

"Megan, that was hours ago," Rick reminded her. "They'd never be able to get down that road now, believe me."

"I don't understand. It was sunny." The room was starting to spin; she leaned her head against the wall and blinked several times.

"We were all surprised," Stanton said. "We would never have driven out here if we had known this would happen."

Megan licked her lips with a dry tongue. She felt as if she had been asleep for days. "What are we going to do now?"

"Stan was just on his way out to see how bad the road is," Rick explained. "But it's dark already, so I don't know if there is anything we can do tonight."

"We have to spend the night here." Megan stated the obvious.

"I'll go have a look around." Stan had zipped up his jacket and was pulling on fur-lined gloves. He had a flashlight tucked under one elbow.

"Be careful, Stan," Rick cautioned.

Megan shivered as she heard the cottage door close behind Stan. "I'm so cold."

"The furnace doesn't seem to be working," Rick said.

Megan remembered the chill in the cottage the day she and Stacie had packed Margaret's clothes. "The pilot light won't stay lit. I remember now."

"How about the fireplace?"

Megan shrugged one shoulder. "I don't know. I was only here in the summer. I never saw Margaret use it."

"I'll take a look."

She heard him shuffling around in the other room. "Looks promising," he called to her, his voice echoing around the empty room. He stuck his head back in the doorway. "Do you suppose there are any matches around?"

"Maybe in the kitchen. I remember Margaret used to have to light the stove. But what are you going to burn?

"I'm not sure. One thing at a time."

Rick rummaged around in the kitchen. Megan heard the cabinet doors opening and closing until he found what he was looking for.

"A fire won't do you any good in the other room," he said when he came back. "We have to move you."

Megan nodded and started to get up. Her head dropped like a boulder into her hands.

Rick knelt next to her on the mattress and put his arms around her. "Don't try to move on your own," he said. "I'll carry you. Can you get your arm around my neck?"

Meekly she obeyed his instructions. With one arm

around her back and the other under her knees, he lifted her off the mattress. She could feel his breath on her face. As he turned to find the doorway, his lips brushed across her cheek.

The couch was the only furniture left in the living room. Gently, Rick set Megan down and helped her to lean back against a throw pillow.

"Are you okay?" he asked anxiously.

Megan nodded. "I think so. My head hurts when I move it, that's all." She closed her eyes and rubbed the fingers of one hand across her forehead. "Rick, I'm so cold. . ."

"Megan, listen to me. Look at me," he demanded, taking her face in his hands and looking straight at her.

She looked up at him, but had trouble focusing her eyes.

"We've got to get you warmed up. I'm going outside to look for firewood. Maybe there's a stack behind the house or somewhere."

"I don't remember. . .any wood. . .," she murmured, wanting only to lay her head back and go to sleep.

"Megan, please, hang on. I'll be right back. I'm only going around the back of the house."

She nodded, and he left. Without the support of his hands, her head fell back heavily against the couch. Behind her closed eyes, a white spinning indistinct image tormented her, disappearing only when she heard a crash. With a flinch she opened her eyes.

Actually the sound was only the cottage door creaking open again. Stanton Phillips entered. Eyeing her, he stomped the snow off his boots and rubbed his hands together.

"You okay?" he asked.

Megan nodded, too tired to speak.

"I saw Rick and said I'd look after you while he looks for wood."

"Thank you," she said, almost inaudibly.

"I have a thermos of coffee," he said. "Do you want some?"

Megan perked up slightly. The thought of a hot drink appealed to her. "Coffee?"

"Yes, coffee. I hope you like it black." He picked up the thermos from the floor next to the door and sat down on the floor beside the couch. When he removed the lid, steam erupted from the thermos with its welcome warmth. He used the lid for a cup and handed her the dark liquid.

"Thank you," she said sincerely. She held the small cup with both hands and breathed in the strong black aroma. When she swallowed a mouthful, she could feel the heat radiating through her chest. "Is it still snowing?"

He nodded. "Heavily. I'm afraid we have no choice but to stay here at least until it's light."

"You must be freezing. Here, you drink this coffee." She offered it to him.

"No, you have it."

Megan did not argue with him; the coffee was too comforting to surrender. She took another swallow.

"It's a lucky thing we found you when we did," he said, straightening the pillow behind her. "Here, lean back. Are you comfortable?"

She nodded. "Just achy and cold."

"If Rick hadn't been a little late for our meeting, he wouldn't have seen your car."

Megan's head was starting to clear once again. "You were having a meeting?" she asked, remembering that Dillon had said no papers had been signed for the sale of the land.

Stan poured more coffee from the thermos into the cup. "Rick is a very talented architect. I'm thinking of investing in his project."

"You are?" Megan was surprised. She had imagined that Stanton Phillips would sell the land and then be out of the picture.

Stan laughed a little. "You sound like you don't think he's got a good idea."

"Well, the idea's okay, I suppose. . ."

"Then you don't believe in Rick's talent?"

"Of course I do," she said, blushing.

"But you're attached to this camp, aren't you?"

This conversation was unlike anything Megan had imagined coming from Stanton Phillips. She wondered if it were real or if she was delirious from her headache. "I think the camp makes a valuable contribution to the community," she said finally.

"I never liked it much, but in theory I can agree with you." He gestured with the thermos. "More?"

She shook her head and handed him the cup. "No, thanks. I feel a little warmer now."

He screwed the lid back on the thermos. "Let me know when you want more. It won't stay hot all night, so you might as well drink it."

To her surprise, he resumed their conversation. "Actually the first year I came here wasn't too bad. It wasn't until my parents came back from Europe that I realized they had sent me here because they didn't want me with them."

In the dim light, Stanton's sharp features looked softer to Megan, and she could almost see the little boy who had come to camp all those years ago and had his heart broken because of it. "I'm sorry you had to go through that," she said.

"When school started that year, they found a boarding school for me," he continued, "a highly respected, elite, pompous school. I was supposed to be grateful to be accepted, I suppose."

"But you would rather have been with your parents?"

He nodded wordlessly, looking away from her. "But I

survived." He tossed the thermos from one hand to the other. "I wonder how Rick is doing?"

The spell broke just when Megan was wishing he would keep talking.

Stan got up and peered out the window into the dark. "I think I see Rick's light. Looks like he's got something in his arms, too."

Megan breathed a sigh of relief that Rick was returning safely. The wind howled and battered the walls of the cottage, an eerie reminder of the blizzard outside. If anything had happened to Rick in the middle of the storm— well, she hated to think about it. Megan shivered and hugged her arms around herself.

Stan watched as the dot of light came closer and grew larger. At the right moment, he opened the door for Rick. An icy blast filled the room, and it took both men to lean on the door and close it securely again.

Rick was uniformly covered with a layer of white that soon began to drip on the carpet. During the moment that the door was open, Megan could see that the snow was rapidly drifting up against the house. The glistening beauty of white expanses earlier in the day had become a damp, dark nightmare.

Rick's arms were filled with assorted pieces of broken timber. "I found a pile of wood pieces under a tarp up by the cabins. Looks like something that got torn down." He crossed the room and emptied his arms into the fireplace.

"It's the cabin that blew down in the tornado last summer." Megan supplied the missing information for Rick. "Brad always meant to cart that rubble away, but he never had time."

"At the moment, I'm glad it's there." Rick started arranging the wood into a neat formation. "I brought as much as I could carry, but I'm sure it won't last the night."

"I remember my aunt used to keep horse blankets around

somewhere," Stan said. "She was the sort that would have been prepared for something like this."

Megan looked up. "In the basement. I remember seeing them next to the furnace a few weeks ago."

Stan left to look for the blankets.

"There's coffee in the thermos," Megan said. "I'm sure he wouldn't mind if you had some."

"Thanks. Let me see if I can get this going first. The wood was covered, but I'm still afraid it might be wet, and I don't really have any good kindling."

He struck a match against one log. It flickered then went out. Rick tried again with a second match, stooping low to blow on the tiny flame. Megan could see how red and chapped his cheeks and hands were from exposure to the outside air. Her heart filled with tenderness as she watched him working so hard to make her more comfortable.

At last he was satisfied that the fire would catch. "I think we've got it going." He sat beside her on the couch, unzipped his wet jacket, and wrapped one arm gently around her shoulder. "Come closer. You should rest now."

Megan obediently laid her head against Rick's chest as if it were the most natural thing in the world. Beneath the softness of his flannel shirt, she felt the muscles in his chest and could hear his heart beating.

He leaned his head down on top of hers and kissed her hair gently. The scent of his closeness comforted her. In only a few moments, she was relaxed and deeply asleep. She didn't stir when Stanton returned and gently spread a blanket over her.

fifteen

Light seeped beneath the window shade and tumbled across Megan's face as she slept. Instinctively, she squeezed her eyes shut tighter against the intrusion. It grew brighter over the next few minutes, pulling her to a reluctant consciousness.

She tried to turn her head away from the light, but the edge of the blanket rubbed across her cheek and made her scowl at its scratchiness. Her mouth was dry and her neck was stiff, but she had slept soundly.

Megan's sleep was always full of dreams, and this night had been no different. Sleeping against Rick's chest, with his arms wrapped around her, she had relived the sweet dreams of their short weeks together. Over and over, in the slow motion of a dream, she woke to look up into his eyes and see tenderness and protection gazing back at her. His nearness brought warmth that flooded over the cold fear of the day before.

Intermittently during the night, this soothing image had been overshadowed by a presence that sometimes seemed like Stanton Phillips but had no face. Whatever it was, it had no physical substance; it was simply something that rushed past them as she and Rick clung to each other. A cold wind would blow through her dream and then turn strangely warm before it dissipated. The shadow would be gone and she would once again be looking into Rick's gray eyes oblivious to the world around her.

Megan was alone on the couch with no concept of how long ago Rick had gotten up. With her eyes still closed, she breathed in deeply; his delicious scent was still in the air around her. She opened her eyes, and with a start, remembered where she was.

The fire had died out hours ago; even the gray and white, paper-thin ashes had grown cold. Although only her face was exposed to the air, Megan could tell the room had chilled. The comfort of her dream was gone; suddenly she felt fearfully alone.

Cautiously, Megan sat up. The stiffness was not as bad as she expected it to be. She turned her head from side to side slowly.

"Rick?" she called. "Rick, are you still here?"

After a second of silence, during which Megan irrationally feared she had been left alone, Rick appeared from the kitchen.

"Good morning, Megan," he said softly. He crossed the room and stood near her. "How do you feel?"

She rubbed her eyes with the heels of her hands. "Better, I think. My head doesn't hurt as much as it did last night. What time is it?"

"About 6:30. You slept a long time."

Megan smiled at the tone of concern in his voice. She had slept well because she had been with him. Even now, she wished he would sit down beside her and hold her again. But she was not ready to say that. "The fire helped. I guess I finally got warmed up." She glanced around the room again. "Where's Stan?"

"Outside. He had some notion about trying to dig out."

"Just how bad is it?" Megan pushed herself to the edge of the couch and craned her neck to see out the window.

"Here, let me help you." Rick came and put his hand under one elbow. She leaned against the welcome support, testing her swollen ankle gingerly. Even wrapped in her thick wool socks, her foot bulged strangely to one side. She winced as soon as her foot made contact with the floor.

"I guess my foot is worse off than my head," Megan admitted.

"You need a doctor, Megan. Your foot could be broken, or you could have a concussion—"

She interrupted him. "Or I could just be bruised up."

"Well, in any case, you can't walk."

Megan had no argument. But what was the alternative? Stay in the deserted cottage, while no one knew where they were, until a dirt road in an unincorporated corner of the county was plowed?

"Do you want to look out and see for yourself?" Rick offered his arm again.

Careful to keep her weight off her bad ankle, Megan leaned on Rick and hopped to the window. When she let the shade spring up, she was unprepared for the intensity of the light. The glare was so bright she saw spots in her eyes. Everything was white; some of the drifts were four feet high.

The path from the house to the parking area was completely obliterated, except for a lone set of footprints—evidence that Stanton Phillips had ventured outside to see if there were any hope of getting the trio out.

Megan's shoulders sagged. "Normally I don't mind winter too much, but this is not my idea of fun."

"We'll get out, Megan."

"Stacie and Brad must be sick with worry—and your sister! Did she know you were coming up here?"

"Yes, Carol knew what my plans were. But I was supposed to be back in town for dinner last night."

"I'd worry about my class, but I suppose school will be cancelled today, anyway."

Rick nodded and smiled. "I like it when you sound sensible."

Megan blushed and looked out the window again. Rick

was standing right behind her, bearing much of her weight against him. A wave of love washed over her and she turned her head slightly toward him.

That was all the signal he needed. Softly, slowly, he began to stroke her tangled hair, smoothing it back away from her face. She did not stop him. She closed her eyes and leaned fully against him, resting her arms on his hand at her waist. The image of his eyes from her dreams floated under her eyelids.

"Megan, I was really scared for you last night," Rick said. "I can't stand the thought of anything happening to you."

"I'm glad you were the one to find me," she said softly. She pivoted on her good foot to face him, her hands resting lightly on his forearms. "Rick, I'm sorry—"

"Shhh," he said, his face close to hers. "Don't worry about anything. We can work things out."

"But I—"

He silenced her with a kiss. As his hands moved to her back to press her closer, she returned the passion of his lips.

The front door opened and they jumped apart. Stanton Phillips blew in with a gust of wind. In one hand he held an old, bent shovel, and in the other was Megan's small wooden sled.

"My sled! How did you get that?" she asked, incredulous.

"Well, first I had to find your car in the snow. Then I had to dig it out. And there was the sled, in the back seat." He set the sled down and propped the snow shovel against the wall. "And here are your keys."

She reached for the keys he dangled in front of her. "Thanks. I never even thought about my keys."

"For obvious reasons." Stan had taken off his gloves and was wiping moisture from his face with his bare hand.

"How did you know she had a sled in the trunk?" Rick asked.

"I saw her put it there yesterday, remember?"

"That sledding trip seems like a lifetime ago," Megan said.

"In retrospect, it was stupid for any of us to come out here, but at least you had the good sense to bring a sled. That's what I call being prepared."

Megan looked at Stanton Phillips with fresh eyes. He was teasing her, and such playfulness was the last thing she would have expected from him under the circumstances. Quickly, she recovered her senses. "But you were the one who remembered I had it."

"This just may be your ticket out of here."

Megan steadied herself on the wall and hopped back to the couch. Her breath hung in the chilled air, even inside the cottage. "I don't know. That sled is pretty rickety," she said, with reservations.

"It seemed to serve you well yesterday," Stan observed.

Megan conceded the point. "Yes, but that was just going down the hill a few times. It's four miles from here to the main road."

"So, we'll pull you," Rick assured her.

"With a twenty-year-old piece of clothesline? What if something happens before we get to the highway?"

Stan laughed. "You sound as if you'd rather stay here!"

"No, of course not, she protested, "but. . ."

"Then stop being quite so sensible!" Rick chastised playfully. "Trust us; we will get you out of here."

"Well, all right. I guess I don't have much choice."

Stan clapped his hands together. "Good. Let's get started."

"Bundle up, Megan," Rick instructed. "We'll never get your boot back on, but we can take the blankets."

Megan fished in her pockets for her gloves and pulled

them on. With Rick's help, she put her good foot in its boot, pulled up her hood, and tied her scarf securely around her neck. Rick zipped up his jacket and pulled a stocking cap down over his head. They looked at each other and smiled, their faces barely visible to each other.

"Ready when you are," Megan said, her extra boot tucked under her arm.

Stan opened the door and set the sled down in the snow outside. Rick scooped up Megan and deposited her on the center of the sled, then wrapped one blanket around her foot and draped the other around her shoulders. He picked up the rope and gave a practice pull. With the first tug, Megan felt her neck protest the motion, but she gave no outward sign of the pain.

"Easy, Rick," Stan said. "You have delicate cargo there."

Rick looked down apologetically at Megan and began to pull with a smoother motion. Stan kept in step beside him.

"Wait!" Stan said suddenly. "We should take the snow shovel." He turned around to go back to the cottage and retrieve their only weapon against the snow.

"If I weren't here, you and Stan could hike out," Megan said, after Stan left. "I'm holding you back."

"Don't be ridiculous."

"He's gone to an awful lot of trouble for me. I mean, digging out my car and remembering the sled and the coffee and blankets last night."

"What did you expect, Megan? You got banged up pretty badly."

"But Stanton Phillips and I haven't exactly gotten off to a great start."

"He's not a monster, Megs. Just an ordinary man with a business to run."

Stan returned just then, so Megan had no chance to answer Rick. "Ready?" Stan asked.

"Ready!" Rick responded, picking up the ragged rope.

The snow crunched beneath their feet as they got off to a jerky start. Megan grasped the sides of the sled with both hands and tried to keep her sore ankle from being jostled too much. She grimaced silently, grateful that Rick and Stan had their back to her and could not see her reaction to the pain in her shoulders and foot. Helpless to contribute to the rescue effort, she determined at least not to make it more difficult.

They reached the gate and turned out onto where they thought the road was; it was nearly impossible to tell. Megan's car was off to one side, its dull red finish a strange sight amid the unceasing spread of white.

Snow hung heavy on the tree branches towering above them. If the scene had been on a Christmas card, it would have seemed picturesque, the classic winter wonderland. In reality, it was something much different. The wind gusted in their faces, and the air was almost too cold to breathe.

For more than an hour, they continued. Stan and Rick took turns pulling the sled. Megan had been down the road more times than either Stan or Rick, so they relied on her recollection of landmarks to navigate.

She wasn't used to seeing everything blanketed in snow and was often unsure of the advice she gave. Constantly, she kept her eyes focused ahead, looking for anything familiar by which to be guided.

"Hey!" she called out suddenly. "Look! A plow!"

She had spotted a flash of yellow and seen a pile of white shift to one side of the road.

Rick and Stan started waving their arms and joined her in yelling at the occupants of the vehicle. In a few moments, they heard the engine growling nearer and knew they would be safe.

A familiar form jumped out of one side of the cab.

"Brad!" Megan exclaimed. "What in the world! Is that Paul's truck with a plow in front?"

"You got it," Brad said. "You gotta admit, Megan, you sure do things in a dramatic way. What in the world happened?"

Stacie and Paul emerged from the truck right behind Brad. "Megan Browning, we've been up all night worrying about you!" Stacie scolded through her tears of relief. She nearly threw herself at Megan, who braced herself for the impact.

"I forgot my scarf," Megan said simply.

"A scarf! You spent the night out here because of a scarf?

"Well, not exactly. . ."

"You were right behind us. What happened?"

"I went back on the hill for my scarf and then I hit some ice and ended up in the ditch and then it was snowing so hard and won't somebody just get me out of here?"

"What she means is," Rick interpreted, "that she got hurt and blacked out and Stan and I found her in the cottage."

"Stan?" Brad said, putting the pieces together.

"Yes," Megan answered. "This is Stan Phillips, who has been very kind to me and without whom I would probably be an icicle by now."

She turned to look at Stan directly. "Thank you, Stan. I don't have words to express my gratitude to you for what you've done."

Brad and Stacie looked on with shocked expressions as they realized Stanton Phillips had befriended Megan, and Megan was responding quite sincerely.

sixteen

Traffic whooshed by in a steady gray drone as Megan dozed gracelessly in the armchair. Her sore ankle, wrapped in a thick support bandage and two socks, was delicately propped up on the coffee table and cushioned with a bed pillow. Her head hung limply to one side of the chair.

The Christmas tape that she had started before sitting down had long ago finished; the little red light on the tape deck vainly beckoned her to come and shut off the power. A mug of coffee, now abandoned and cold, sat on the table next to her foot. A magazine had slipped from her lap into the crevice of the chair. Megan had not meant to fall asleep in the middle of Wednesday morning.

It was not a deep sleep. Megan was vaguely aware of the outside noises, muffled by the closed windows of winter, and of Franklin nuzzling her leg, looking for attention. For several minutes, she had been feeling chilled and wished she had put on a sweater.

Somehow the apartment felt cooler when she was sitting still, or perhaps in her half-dream state she was feeling the frigid air of the unheated cottage once again. She shivered both against the chill and the haunting thought.

Shaking her head briskly and stretching her eyes open wide, Megan leaned down and scooped up Franklin.

"Here we are, my friend," she said aloud. "One old gray cat and one sorry klutz." Smoothly and slowly, she stroked his back, and he nestled into her lap, content.

"I don't suppose you could go get my sweater." Franklin made no response. Megan leaned her head back again, feeling too relaxed to get up and move around.

Her thoughts went to her classroom, already festively arrayed for the holidays, and the fifty-three kindergartners in her morning and afternoon sessions whom she would not see again until after New Year's.

Her ankle was not broken, but it was badly sprained. The doctor had kept her at the hospital overnight for observation because of the bump on her head and then forbidden her to go back to work for at least two weeks. By then, it would be the middle of Christmas vacation.

She had no choice but to accept that a substitute would take her place for the days remaining until the winter break began. She hoped she would at least be able to limp to the Christmas program the children had prepared for so earnestly.

A rap on the door startled her. She jumped slightly before calling out, "Who is it?"

"Me!"

"Rick! Hi, I'll be right there."

She nudged the reluctant Franklin out of her lap and took a moment to strategize her next move. The crutches Rick had insisted she accept from the doctor were leaning against the back of the couch, just out of her reach. Carefully she took her foot off the coffee table, pulled herself to an upright position. and hopped over to the crutches.

She was sure she could have reached the door without the crutches, but she knew she would never hear the end of it if Rick caught her without them.

Disheveled but radiant, she hobbled to the door and turned the deadbolt. "Hi," she said, casually tilting her face up for the kiss she knew he would give.

"Hi yourself." He delivered not just a simple hello kiss but took her in his arms for a warm, moist, it's-been-too-long-since-I've-seen-you kiss that left her nearly breathless.

"Mmm," she purred, "I like that."

"We aim to please." Rick smiled down at her, still not releasing his hold on her. "Let's get you off your feet."

Without protesting, she leaned against him and let him lead her to the couch. But before dropping into the middle cushion, she spied her coffee mug again. "Would you like some coffee?" she asked, reaching for her mug. "Mine's cold."

"A cup of coffee would be great, but I'll get it."

"I can manage. I got my own earlier."

"Megan, don't make me scold you," he teased. "Sit down." He put his hands squarely on her shoulders and pushed just hard enough to make her fall backward into the couch.

"Well, okay, but don't put so much sugar in mine this time."

"Yes, ma'am." He took her mug from her hand and disappeared into the small kitchen.

"There are some doughnuts on the counter, too, if you want them," she called.

"Thanks, I see them."

Rick reappeared after a moment with two mugs of steaming coffee and the box of doughnuts. He set everything down on the table.

"Is this breakfast?" he asked suspiciously, gesturing toward the doughnuts.

"The one a couple hours ago was," she confessed. Megan considered the remaining selection while Rick scowled. "Hey, I'm entitled to a little self-indulgence."

"Well. . .all right, considering the circumstances."

"How's Stan?" Megan asked, having won her point. She took a deep breath and savored the aroma of black coffee.

"He's fine. He's on his way back to California." Rick

settled onto the couch beside her.

"California? He left?"

Rick nodded. "He's leaving everything up to his lawyer to handle. After all, he has a business to run in LA."

"I suppose so. I didn't know he was going so soon. I wanted to thank him again for all his help last Sunday and Monday."

"He knows you appreciate it." Rick smiled. "I'm sorry you got hurt, and I would never have chosen to get caught unprepared by a snowstorm. But I'm glad you got a chance to see that Stan is not the monster you thought he was."

"I never thought he was a monster," Megan quickly said in her own defense. "I just thought he didn't appreciate the Homestead like he should."

Rick's expression sobered. "Speaking of the Homestead, Stan's lawyer called me this morning. He said he's had another inquiry about the land."

Megan's heart quickened, and her coffee sloshed with her sudden nervousness. "Someone else is interested in buying it?"

Rick nodded. "I'm afraid so."

Megan knew the inquiry must have been from Dillon Graves. How much should she tell Rick? "I thought you had a deal with Stan."

"I do. At least I think I do. But technically we haven't signed anything yet."

"So if someone should outbid you. . ."

"Stan's a businessman. He would probably take the better offer."

"Why haven't you signed a sales contract yet?" Megan asked.

"When the property went on the market, Stan decided he would take bids until December 31 and then finalize the sale after that."

Megan looked away from Rick while she thought about the implications of this information. December 31. That was Brad and Stacie's wedding day. That meant Dillon had only three weeks to try to raise enough money to buy the camp.

Rick grew suspicious of her distractedness. "Megan," he said, "do you know something you're not telling me?"

"What do you mean?" She evaded his question and took a bite of a doughnut.

"I can see your eyes flashing," he pressed her. "I haven't known you long, but I know you well.

Megan kept chewing.

"Are you still hoping I won't be able to buy the land? You know, I'm not the only developer around. If this other buyer gets the land, you don't know what will happen to the camp."

She debated what to say. Should she tell Rick she knew who the buyer was? If he knew, would he be able to do anything to foil Dillon's plans?

"Megan?"

"You're right; there is something I haven't told you." She paused, looking for the right words. "Dillon Graves is thinking of making an offer on the land."

"Dillon Graves? That guy who was at Stacie's on Thanksgiving?"

"Yes. Stacie works with him."

"I remember. Is he serious?"

Megan nodded. "I think so."

"Does he really have that kind of money?"

"He's trying to raise it; he's talking with investors, just like you are."

Rick was skeptical. "How can he find anyone to invest in that old camp?"

Megan got defensive. "There are plenty of people around

who believe that a kids' camp is a very worthwhile thing. And Dillon thinks he can make the place profitable."

"And you hope he can do it." It was a statement, not a question. Rick knew how she felt about the camp.

She didn't deny it. "You know how I feel about that place. If Dillon buys it, he plans to keep running the camp."

"I know that would make you happy," Rick said, putting his coffee mug down and sinking back into the couch. "But what about my dream? This is a great opportunity for me."

Megan was prepared to assert herself. Since the night at the cottage and their reunion, she had thought long and hard about how she would handle this moment.

"Rick," she said, "you know I love you. I tried to ignore my feelings for you, but I can't. But I can't ignore my feelings about the Homestead, either. You said a couple weeks ago that one thing was business and the other personal, and they didn't have anything to do with each other."

"Well, I know, but—"

"Let me finish." She swallowed and continued slowly and deliberately. "At first I didn't think it was possible to separate the two—and I'm still not sure that it is. But you wanted me to try, so I've decided to try. You have to know that I'll be supporting Dillon's effort to raise money."

Megan paused to study his strained and sober expression. "That doesn't mean that I don't care about you, but it's how I feel."

"I see." Rick stood up and started pacing around the room. "How much money has Dillon got?"

Megan shook her head. "That's not a fair question. I haven't asked you how much you've offered to pay for the land."

"Point taken." Rick tried another tactic. "Can you tell me if he has anyone seriously interested in investing? Or is he going to try to get a mortgage for part of the price?"

Megan reached out over the back of the couch and caught Rick's hand to stop his nervous movements. "Rick, I've told you all I'm going to tell you. And I'm not going to tell Dillon anything, either. I'm not in the spy business.

Rick stared into her brown eyes with his own gray ones. "I believe you, and that seems fair." He squeezed her hand. "So what do we do now?"

Megan shrugged. "So far we've always managed to find other things to talk about. I don't want it to come between us any more than you do."

"Okay. That's the end of it." Rick sighed. Never letting go of her hand, he circled around the couch and sat next to her again. He had a sly smile on his lips. "I'm sure we'll find some other diversion."

Megan blushed and swallowed the last of her coffee. "Whatever do you have in mind?"

He stroked her cheek with the back of his hand. "Oh, let's see; there's feeding Franklin."

"I did that already." She inched closer to him.

"I saw some dirty dishes in your kitchen sink," he continued, putting his arm around her shoulder.

"They can wait." She leaned her head back on his shoulder and snuggled against him.

They sat quietly for a moment as he stroked her hair and kissed the top of her head. But somehow Megan knew she did not have his full attention.

"I don't think Dillon can do it," Rick said in evidence of his preoccupation. "He doesn't have enough time to raise the money. I'm sure Stan will sell to me."

"Rick Avery!" She slapped his stomach playfully and pulled away from him. "I thought we had a deal."

"You're right." He pulled her back close. "I may not be able to stop thinking about it, but I promise not to talk about it."

He kissed her affectionately.

"That's more like it," she said.

"Like I said earlier, we aim to please."

He wrapped his arms tightly around her and gave her the attention she was looking for.

seventeen

Three hours later, Rick reluctantly admitted that he had to get back to work. While he was waiting for his deal with Stanton Phillips to finalize, Rick had accepted some freelance architectural work for a commercial developer.

He hoped it would be the last time he worked for someone else, but he had to make a living. Although he could take a few hours off during the day, eventually he had to face the reality of his end-of-the-week deadline. After all it was a workday, even if Megan had been ordered to stay home by the doctor.

"I'm going to fix you a decent meal before I go," he said.

Megan raised an eyebrow. "No doughnuts for lunch?"

"No doughnuts for lunch," he admonished firmly.

Rick disappeared into the kitchen and Megan listened, amused, at the clinking sounds of dishes and the creaking cabinet doors. When he returned, he had two ham and cheese sandwiches, a generous supply of carrot sticks, an apple, and the tallest glass she owned filled to the brim with milk.

"I don't usually eat this much lunch," she said.

"You need extra fortification."

"You're fussing over me."

"Are you complaining?" He set the plate squarely in front of her.

"I'm not used to it."

"Well, get used to it. I'm a creature of habit." He picked up his jacket. "I made a fresh pot of coffee, too."

With that, Rick left her alone for the afternoon. His scent

lingered in the air, and with it his presence. She did not have to reach for Franklin to avoid feeling lonely. Rick was with her even when he was not there. More and more, Megan liked the feeling of being in love.

After a few moments, she ate the lunch he'd left, grateful for his earlier insistence. After devouring both sandwiches—to her own surprise—she crunched the apple contentedly. If Rick wanted to pamper her, why should she object? It would just take some getting used to; she was used to looking out for herself.

She was also used to being more active. After two days cooped up in her apartment, the limitations of her sore ankle were frustrating her. It was bad enough that she could not go to work; but not being able to get to another room comfortably was particularly irritating. She still had a lot of Christmas shopping to do, and she wanted to find the perfect wedding gift for Brad and Stacie.

Out of desperation she limped over to the bookcase and pulled the Sears catalogue off the bottom shelf, out from underneath a stack of construction paper. Many of the pages had holes where she had cut pictures out for some school project, but there was plenty to look at. Flipping through the catalogue might at least inspire some ideas, and hopefully she would be able to be up and around in another few days.

With the catalogue and a novel that had been on her want-to-read list for a long time, Megan passed the afternoon quite pleasantly. She did not even realize that it had grown dark outside.

For the second time that day, a knock on the door startled her.

"Who is it?"

"Room service."

"Stacie? Is that you?"

"Open up."

"I'm coming, I'm coming." She got up and hobbled toward the door. "These things take time."

When she pulled the door open, Stacie thrust three small white boxes at her.

"Chinese food?" Megan asked, scrunching up her face with the question.

"Yes. Dinner. I'm here to make sure you're eating properly."

"You too?" Megan muttered under her breath.

"What's that?" Stacie asked.

"Never mind." Megan turned around to shuffle back to her chair.

"Why is it so dark in here?" Stacie asked as she turned on a lamp.

Megan shrugged. "I didn't notice."

"You weren't reading, were you?" Stacie scolded. "Your mother would tell you not to read in the dark."

"I don't need my mother," Megan retorted playfully. "I have you."

"How's your foot?"

"Sore, but getting better."

"You're not going to be on crutches at my wedding, are you?"

"Relax, Stacie. The doctor said I should be fine by then—at least well enough to glide gracefully down the aisle ahead of the blushing bride."

Stacie made a sour face at Megan's sarcasm and started unpacking the food. "We have egg rolls, sweet and sour pork, and of course, plenty of rice." She handed Megan a set of chopsticks.

"Sounds scrumptious." Megan dropped heavily into her armchair. "But all I've done today is sit and eat." She gestured toward the lunch dishes still cluttering the coffee table. "Rick insisted I eat enough lunch for four people."

"Rick was here?"

"Yes," Megan answered guardedly. She had detected an uncomfortable tone in Stacie's voice. "He came by to check on me this morning."

"Check on you? Is that all?" Stacie bit into an egg roll.

Megan set down her chopsticks. "Stacie, we've known each other too long to play games. What are you getting at?"

Stacie shrugged. "Nothing, really. I was just wondering..." Her sentence drifted off, unfinished.

"If Rick and I are back together?" Megan pressed the point that Stacie was reluctant to verbalize. "Well, we are."

"Oh." Stacie took another bite.

Megan still had not started eating, and now she felt less hungry than ever. "You don't like that Rick and I are back together, do you?"

"It's not really up to me."

"Rick is important to me. I'd like your support."

Stacie stopped eating and turned slowly toward Megan. "Well," she said, fishing for words, "not too long ago you said you and Rick were just too different from each other, that you wanted different things."

"And I was miserable," Megan pointed out. "You saw for yourself."

"What changed?"

"I have a different perspective on things now."

"Something spectacular must have happened while you were snowed in."

Megan shook her head. "It wasn't anything spectacular. But when I opened my eyes and saw Rick, I was so glad he was there. I realized that I *wanted* him to be there. I could have gone on being stubborn and miserable apart from him—I was doing my best to avoid him.

"But there we were, thrown together. I'm not wild about this sore ankle or the bump on my head, but something good came out of that snowstorm."

Megan reached for the egg roll and busied herself inspecting it while waiting for Stacie to respond.

Stacie took a slow bite of pork. "Megan, I only want what's best for you. After breaking up with Brad and then getting back together again, I'd be a hypocrite to insist you have to stick with your original decision. I just don't want you to get hurt."

"No one can guarantee that, Stace."

"But what about the camp and Rick's project and all that stuff?"

"Rick and I have a new agreement," Megan announced with a note of triumph.

"Oh?"

"He wants me to separate business from personal, so I will. I'll keep seeing him, but he knows about Dillon's bid on the camp and he knows that I'm supporting Dillon."

"And that's all right with Rick?"

Megan laughed softly. "No, it's not all right. But he's agreed to it. How could he argue? He's the one who suggested putting things in separate compartments in the first place."

Stacie smiled back at Megan. "You're smooth, Megan, very smooth."

"Rick tried to pump me for information about Dillon, but I didn't say anything. And I won't tell Dillon anything about Rick, either. I'm keeping my nose clean."

Stacie's shoulders sagged. "Well, there may not be much to tell, anyway."

"What do you mean?" Megan had started eating quite energetically and spoke with her mouth full.

"Dillon is running out of time."

Megan nodded. "Rick said Stan is only accepting bids until December 31."

Stacie drew back, surprised. "Stan? You're calling that

man by his first name now?"

Megan waved a hand at her friend. "Knock it off. He is just a man, and not so nasty as we made him out to be."

"I guess he was pretty nice to you," Stacie admitted grudgingly.

"More than nice," Megan corrected. "But tell me more about Dillon. Isn't he making any progress?"

Stacie tilted her head to one side thoughtfully. "Oh, some, I guess. But he's the type who is eternally optimistic, and I'm not so sure he's making enough progress."

"Just what does he say?"

"He's got about twenty-five percent of the money that he needs. He could never get a mortgage on that much property on his salary, so he has to raise virtually all the money."

"Three weeks is not much time."

Stacie shook her head in silent agreement. "If only he could have a few more weeks, then maybe he could do it."

"He must be burning the candle at both ends, between getting ready to open the new shelter and trying to find investors for the camp."

"He is," confirmed Stacie, "and it all might be for nothing. Even if he reaches his goal, there's no way to be sure it will be enough to outbid Rick." She looked at Megan with wide questioning green eyes.

Megan put her hands up in a defensive gesture. "Hey, don't look at me. I'm staying out of it, remember? I'll do what I can for Dillon, short of overt sabotage."

"You're right, of course," said Stacie, turning her attention back to her food. "But you have to admit, you are in a strategic position to influence what happens."

"How's Brad?" Megan asked, deliberately changing the subject. "Does he still think you're overdoing it with the wedding plans?"

Whether conscious of it or not, Stacie took the bait and chattered on about various details of wedding preparations: who should be seated at which table for the reception, whether Brad's four-year-old niece would cooperate as the flower girl, whether she should use the church's candelabra or rent some better ones.

Megan smiled pleasantly and nodded her head as Stacie recounted each of these dilemmas, offering observations where she could but generally just letting Stacie blow off some of her frustrations. The evening was passing quickly.

"Oh my!" Stacie exclaimed when she finally looked at her watch at 7:30. "I'm supposed to meet Brad to go Christmas shopping for his mother. I gotta go." She started gathering up the paper boxes with leftovers. "I'll put this stuff in your fridge so you won't have to cook tomorrow."

"Thanks."

Stacie vanished into the kitchen with the Chinese food and miscellaneous dishes.

"Maybe I should stay and do your dishes," Stacie called out to Megan.

"Don't bother. I can sit on a stool to do them."

"Are you sure?" Stacie reappeared in the living room.

"Positive. Would you get out of here, please?"

"Do you need anything else? I could come by again in the morning. Groceries or anything?"

"I think I'm well stocked," Megan responded. "Now get going, or Brad will have my head for making you late."

"Okay, I'm going, but call me if you need anything."

Megan dutifully promised to make her needs known and hopped to the door to escort Stacie out. She bolted the door shut and then leaned against it. Franklin, who had left the room as soon as Stacie arrived, now floated past her in his snobbish, mysterious way.

"Well, Franklin, finally some peace and quiet, eh? Bet you're glad she's gone." She hobbled back to the couch and patted the cushion beside her. "Come on, boy, don't give me the cold shoulder just because I have friends and you don't."

Franklin obliged by leaping up onto the couch and snuggling against Megan with all four white paws up in the air. As she rubbed his belly lightly with her fingertips, Megan's eyes wandered to the telephone, and she wondered if Rick would remember his promise to call.

It was still early, she reminded herself. Even if he didn't call for another two hours, they would have plenty of time to talk. But maybe he was busy with his free-lance project and did not have time for a pleasant but purposeless conversation with a housebound kindergarten teacher.

"I'm tired of sitting on this stupid couch," she said aloud.

Franklin twitched his whiskers but otherwise did not move.

"Sorry, Franklin, the pampering is over. I'm going to do the dishes." With Rick still on her mind, she reached for the crutches propped against one end of the couch and pulled herself up.

In the kitchen, she scooted a bar stool up to the sink and perched on it. She snapped on the radio and twirled the dial to find some lively music and set about her task of cleaning up the dishes. Between the radio and her own singing, she almost didn't hear the phone ring, and it took her several rings to reach it.

"Hello?" she said breathlessly.

"Hi there," came the familiar warm tones she had been waiting for.

eighteen

The organ burst forth in a triumphant recessional of "Joy to the World!" Megan uninhibitedly hummed along and watched as the red glass balls on the Christmas tree in the front of the sanctuary twinkled their reflection of the lights overhead.

Contentedly, she turned in the pew and smiled up at Rick. In response, he offered his arm. She linked her arm through his, discretely allowing him to bear some of her weight, and they began the walk up the center aisle of the church.

Megan raised her eyes to the festive red and white banners hanging from the balcony. "I love this time of year," she said. "The decorations, the music—I love it all. I'm always so disappointed when Christmas is over."

"But you haven't even put up a tree," protested Rick.

Megan glanced down at her bad ankle. "Well, it's been a little hard for me to get out."

"Why didn't you say something about it?" he prodded.

Megan shrugged. "You've been taking such good care of me already. A Christmas tree seemed like too much to ask for."

"Don't be silly. We'll do it today."

"Really?" Megan squealed like a delighted child and squeezed his arm. "Can we?"

Rick laughed. "Sure. I saw some nice looking ones only a few blocks from here."

Rick fetched their coats and left Megan standing in the narthex while he went for his car. She insisted she could walk to the car—although slowly—but he would not hear of it. Gallantly, he pulled right up to the front door of the church, opened the car door, and let her lean on him as she lowered herself into the seat.

It had not snowed again since the blizzard had trapped them in the cottage a week earlier. But neither had it warmed up, so the frozen and frosty evidence of that weekend was all around them. Evergreen limbs hung low under the weight of several inches of show. Rotund snowmen in odd proportions dotted the neighborhood around the church.

The streets and most of the sidewalks were clear. After plowing out from the surprise blizzard, St. Mary's had gone about its usual business like all the hardy Midwestern towns around it.

The imminence of the holidays spurred people out to the shopping centers despite the snow. Joyous that the long-awaited Christmas vacation had arrived, children were lying on the ground making joyous snow angels and stockpiling snowballs to hurl at unsuspecting adults and passing cars.

Rick cautiously pulled out of the parking lot as a snowball splatted against his windshield. "You know," he said, "in some parts of the country there is never snow at Christmas."

Megan thought the comment was an odd one. "Are you thinking of Stan, in California?"

Rick shook his head. "Not in particular. I'm just making the observation that Christmas is not always the picture postcard that it is around here."

"Oh." Megan was too puzzled by what he was getting at to respond further. They drove several blocks in silence.

"Have you ever thought about living in another part of the country?" Rick asked.

"Where it doesn't snow, you mean?"

"Just anywhere. Anywhere but here."

Megan still did not know what he was getting at. "I suppose. But I've always been pretty happy in the Midwest. My family is only four hours away, and I have a lot of friends here."

"And a good job," offered Rick.

"A wonderful job," she agreed, quickly, "and a terrific principal."

"I suppose it would be hard for you to move away from all that." Rick flipped the turn signal and steered the car toward the left. "I think those Christmas trees I saw were down this way."

Was he changing the subject? Megan wondered. She had not even been sure what the subject was. When he glanced over at her, she smiled but did not speak.

They pulled into the lot where the Boy Scouts were selling trees. Rick parked the car and came around to open Megan's door, as he always did when they were out together.

"How's the foot?" he asked as she carefully swung her legs out the door and stood up.

"Not too bad actually. I just have to take it slow." She took his hand and they walked toward the trees.

"How big a tree do you want?" he asked. "A tabletop?"

"Oh, no!" Megan protested. "I want the real thing. Six feet at least."

"Where are you going to put it?" Rick was skeptical.

"I'll find a place. I did last year."

He shrugged in surrender. "Okay." He gestured toward the trees. "What's your pleasure?"

They meandered through the maze of trees, evaluating fullness and dryness and height.

"Most of these trees look fairly fresh," Megan observed.

Rick nodded. "I guess in some parts of the country, they have to truck them in from thousands of miles away."

"What places?" Megan asked, her curiosity piqued again.

"Oh, you know. Places where they don't have evergreen trees."

"Oh. Those places." She turned her attention to a promising prospect. "This one looks pretty good."

Rick reached through the branches to grasp the tree's trunk and hold it up straight.

"Turn it around," Megan instructed. "Does it have any bare spots?"

"It's a little flat on one side, but the branches will probably drop when it's standing upright."

"Let's take it!" Megan made her decision enthusiastically. "It looks sturdy enough that even Franklin won't pull it over."

Rick insisted on paying for the tree, over Megan's protests, and loaded it bottom end first in the trunk of his car.

There was no more talk of places where Christmas had no snow or trees had to be trucked across the country. But Megan did not stop wondering what those snatches of conversation had really been about.

Was Rick thinking of moving away? Was he going to give up on buying the camp and go back to Pennsylvania? She dismissed that theory, because Pennsylvania had plenty of snow and trees. Rick was definitely talking about some other place: the South perhaps, or the West.

The thought of his leaving put a knot in her throat. But he had asked how *she* felt about living somewhere else. Her heart skipped a beat as she wondered if he was working up to a proposal. Had she sounded too stubborn about not leaving the Midwest? Had she spoken too quickly, without thinking about the consequences?

She waited for him to bring the subject up again, but he seemed to have moved on. The moment had passed. They reached her apartment with very little conversation.

Megan limped up the stairs—the most painful motion for her ankle—holding doors open for Rick as best she could. He had a firm grip on the trunk of the tree and made steady progress. In only a few minutes, they were upstairs in her apartment, tree and all.

"Now I want to see this miracle you're going to perform," he teased.

"No miracle," she said, "just careful planning. If I move this table away from the window and push the chair over that way, there should be plenty of room right here near the door."

"I don't know," Rick said, shaking his head. "Looks awfully tight to me."

"Just try it," she insisted, and he complied. "I'll get the tree stand."

Megan held the tree upright while Rick tightened the bolts into the trunk. Arms around each other—and tripping over displaced furniture—they stood back to admire the bare tree.

"Good choice, Megan," Rick said. "The place will smell like pine in no time."

"Wait till we get the ornaments on."

"Where are they? I'll get them."

She directed him to a large battered cardboard box on the floor of her bedroom closet. When he returned, she eagerly started laying out the ornaments she had gathered since childhood.

"That's quite a collection," he said admiringly.

"I've been saving them since I was eight," Megan explained. "My mother still sends me a new one every year. It's sort of a family tradition."

Rick fingered a hand-painted porcelain trio of carolers with their mouths frozen open in perpetual song. "This is really pretty."

"That was the first one—and still my favorite, I think."

"I like the tradition. I'd like your mother, I'm sure."

Megan took the ornament from him and hung it at the center of the tree, still haunted by their earlier conversation. "Do you suppose they have traditions there?" she asked.

"Where?"

"You know. In those places where they have no snow for Christmas."

"Oh, maybe." He held a delicately carved, wooden angel.

"What year was this from?"

"Two years ago."

"It's nice. So much detail for something so tiny." He gently hung it on an upper branch.

"So?" Megan pressed impatiently.

"So what?"

Megan had had enough. "Frederick Avery, you tell me what's going on right this minute!"

"What are you talking about?"

She snatched a tiny glass church out of his hands. "All this talk about other parts of the country. Are you leaving St. Mary's?"

"Maybe."

Her heart sank and soared at the same time. She did not want him to leave. But if he left, it meant he would not buy the camp and Dillon would have a better chance at the sale.

"Megan, let's sit down for a few minutes." He took her by the hand and led her to the couch. "Let me tell you the whole story."

"Finally!"

He smiled at her mock exasperation. "I had a phone call from Stanton Phillips yesterday."

"And?"

"And he's interested in investing in my project."

"The condominium? I thought he just wanted to sell the land."

"So did I." Rick settled in more comfortably on one corner of the couch. "But I showed him my model while he was here, and he was quite interested. I could really use his financial backing to make this project succeed."

"I still don't get it. What does this have to do with living in another part of the country?"

"That's the catch. Stan has another piece of property in Arizona that he thinks would be better suited to my plans."

"Arizona! That's two thousand miles from here."

Rick nodded soberly. "I know. But what he says makes a lot of sense. The parcel is a little larger, and it's located in an area that is already being developed. In a place like Arizona, I could add a lot of recreational facilities that would really make the units sell."

"I suppose so," Megan murmured.

"I wouldn't have the re-zoning question that I'd have to face here," Rick continued, "and I could cater to buyers who might be looking for a place to spend the winter."

Megan simply nodded.

"I think I can swing the money to buy the land here, but I'd have to do some fast talking to get money to start building."

"Stan won't help if you decide to stay here?"

Rick shook his head. "Nope. That's the condition of his offer. He's convinced that I would be more successful in Arizona."

"It's generous of him to offer to back you."

"He's a shrewd businessman, I'm convinced of that. I would do well to follow the advice of someone like Stan."

"Sounds like you have lots of good reasons to do it, then."

"The problem is, I sort of got used to the idea of staying in St. Mary's."

Megan looked into his eyes without speaking. The tenderness she saw told her that she was the reason he hesitated about Stan's offer.

As much as she hated to think of his leaving, she would not hold him back. The future of the camp was no longer between them. She wanted to give him the support he deserved.

"I think you should do it," she said decisively.

"But..." Rick was not sure what to say.

She patted his knee affectionately. "Rick, this sounds like the best offer you could hope for. You've been wanting this for a long time."

"Will you come?"

"Will I come?" she echoed in disbelief. Did he mean what she thought he meant?

"Will you come with me? To a place where Christmas has no snow and you have to settle for a flattened, dried up tree?"

"Rick, I. . ." It was Megan's turn to be speechless.

"I know it might be hard for you to find another teaching job, and we'll be a long way from your family. But you can fly back for visits, or they can come and see us. Brad and Stacie, too, if you want them to—"

"Shh!" She put her finger on his lips to stop the barrage of words. "Is this an official proposal?"

"Not a very good one," he answered sheepishly.

"It's the thought that counts. Of course I'll come."

nineteen

Rick stayed until late in the evening.

With a new shyness, they smiled at each other over the ornaments they were hanging on the tree. When they finished the decorating, they realized they had never stopped for lunch.

Megan was content to put her sore foot up and let Rick make her a cheese omelet. She was too excited to care about food, but going through the motions of cooking and eating seemed to be a good way to stay connected with the real world. She so easily could have slipped into the romantic fantasy world Stacie accused her of being so fond of.

After the dishes were cleaned up, they built a roaring fire and snuggled on the couch together. It was a magical winter evening, and Megan moaned when Rick finally refused to put another log on the fire and said he had to go.

By the next morning, the spell had broken, and Megan was ready to share her news with the outside world. She waited until she was sure Stacie would be at the office and then phoned.

"You're kidding!" Stacie could not believe Megan's news. "Rick is pulling out? Giving up on the camp?"

"Yes and no." Megan settled into a comfortable chair. "He's going ahead with his project, just with another piece of property." She went on to give a full explanation of Stanton Phillips's offer to invest in Rick's project if he would agree to build in Arizona and Rick's decision to accept the offer.

"Arizona!" exclaimed Stacie. "I know you're excited that the camp won't be turned into condominiums, but I would have thought you'd be more disappointed that Rick is moving so far away. Won't you miss him?"

"No, I won't miss him," Megan said casually.

"I'm confused. I thought Rick was your Mr. Right. How can you let him pick up and move two thousand miles away?"

"Because I'm going with him."

"Megan! Really?"

"He asked me to marry him, and I said yes."

"Oh, Meggers, that's great," Stacie squealed. Then she sobered. "But I'm not so crazy about having you that far away from me. How will I survive without you?"

"Oh, don't sound so pitiful. We're all grown up now. Besides, this is the age of telephones and airplanes."

"It won't be the same," Stacie moped.

"Well, it's not going to happen for a few months, anyway."

"I'm allowed to pout."

Megan smiled and changed the subject. "We'll have plenty of time to talk about that later. The camp is what is important right now. You have to talk to Dillon right away."

"He's not in the office this morning."

"As *soon* as he comes in, you grab him and tell him the news."

"Actually, I don't know if it matters that much."

"What do you mean?" Megan asked.

"I don't think Dillon is having much luck at raising the money he needs. Frankly, I don't see how he can do it by the deadline."

"Have you ever heard of something called a miracle?"

"That's what it would take," Stacie said skeptically. "I

know he's been working on it night and day, but he doesn't say a lot about it. I just get the idea that it's not going so well."

"We have to keep hoping and praying."

"If Rick drops out, does Dillon have any other competition?" asked Stacie.

"I don't know," Megan answered. "Even if there are no other offers, he still has to make a strong bid. If the offer is too low, Stan could decide to leave the property on the market until he gets the price he wants."

"That's true, but at least Dillon might have more time to arrange the financing."

"Now there's a glimmer of hope."

Megan heard a familiar click and was not surprised at Stacie's next remark. "My other line is ringing. I gotta go."

"Call me after you talk to Dillon," Megan insisted.

"I promise."

Megan replaced the receiver in its cradle and sunk deeper into the chair with the phone in her lap. She had told Stacie that there would be plenty of time to talk about her engagement to Rick later, but she herself could not stop thinking about it.

The truth was that Megan had never traveled west of the Mississippi River. She envisioned Arizona as barren desert, punctuated by cactus and blanketed with sand. An image formed in her mind of the casual Southwestern decorating themes that she saw in magazines at the grocery store checkout counters. Is that what her future home would be like—full of purple hues and pointed shapes?

Nostalgically, she looked around her cozy apartment. Yes, it was old and it was small, but it was her home. Here she was securely surrounded by familiar things: her books, her craft pile, her mother's old dishes, her mismatched refinished furniture. Would any of these things have a place in her new life?

She would miss her classroom at Barton Elementary. It represented her first success as a teacher. Some of her students would stay in her heart her whole life. But if Carol became her sister-in-law, she would always have news of what was going on at the school. And she would miss the church she had joined six years ago as a college student, where she had made her first independent decision to live out the values her parents had instilled in her.

But her life was moving forward now. Just as Stacie said, the flip side of Megan's sensibility was hopeless romanticism. She had always wanted to be married; she just never thought it would really happen. But it was. She and Rick had talked about a summer wedding, after she finished out the school year. They might have to be apart for some of the spring months while he began work on his new project, but after that they could always be together.

Megan started checking off a mental list of everything she would have to do to get ready. Her landlord would need to know that she would not be renewing her lease; the school board would need her resignation. She was going to need boxes and boxes for all her stuff. And of course, the wedding!

It seemed unreal that she would be planning her own wedding after agonizing through the process with Stacie. Would she be as particular about everything? Would the shade of the color of the candles matter as much to her as it did to Stacie?

"The shoe's on the other foot now," she said aloud to Franklin, who had jumped up in her lap. She set the phone aside and obliged the cat with a tummy rub. "What about you, Franklin? How do you feel about Arizona?"

"Meow" was all the reply she got.

"I know, Franklin, you're not too sure you even like Rick. But he's not such a bad guy. Actually he's a pretty neat guy if you give him half a chance."

Franklin remained unimpressed.

"I always thought St. Mary's felt like home, after so many years here." Out of habit, Megan kept talking despite Franklin's disinterest. "But that's changed. Now I think that wherever Rick is—that's home for me."

Promptly at five o'clock the doorbell rang. Megan disengaged herself from the laundry she was sorting on the bedroom floor and limped to the door. Peering through the peephole, she saw the distorted faces of Stacie, Brad, and Dillon.

"What are you guys doing here?" she asked as she pulled open the door.

"Strategy meeting." Stacie's reply was cut and dry.

"Pizza is on the way," Brad added.

"They kidnapped me and made me come," was Dillon's innocent contribution to the explanation.

Megan was glad she had confined her dirty laundry to the bedroom earlier that day.

"Well, okay, you can come in, but I'm not paying for the pizza." She stood aside and let them pass. One by one they brushed the branches of the Christmas tree, rattling the ornaments and dragging strings of tinsel across the room.

"Gee, Megan, couldn't you have gotten a bigger tree?" Brad asked.

"Oh hush," she said, slapping his shoulder. "No one invited you here."

The intruders dumped their jackets in a corner and plopped down on the furniture. Stacie rapped her knuckles on the coffee table. "This meeting is hereby called to order."

Amused, Megan propped herself on one arm of the couch. "Madame Chairman, may I have the floor?"

"You may speak."

"I wish to know the purpose and agenda of this meeting."

"I'll answer that," Brad said. "We have assembled this august body in order to consider the financial challenges faced by one of our esteemed members, Mr. Dillon Graves, inasmuch as we share a common interest in the future of the Old Homestead Youth Camp."

Dillon nearly rolled out of his chair with laughter. "You're pretty good with the mumbo jumbo for a carpenter!"

Stacie dropped the formality. "Seriously, now. We've got to find some money!"

The doorbell rang.

"But first," said Brad thrusting his forefinger into the air, "we must eat the ceremonial meal." He got up and opened the door to the pizza delivery man. Before Megan could protest, Stacie shot into the kitchen for plates and a stack of napkins.

"Pepperoni and black olives, and sausage and mushrooms."

As Brad opened the pizza boxes, the aroma attacked Megan and she was instantly ravenous. Before she knew it, she was crouched at the coffee table trying not to get mozzarella cheese all over her face. But she had not forgotten why the group had invaded her apartment.

"So, Dillon, just how is the fund-raising going?"

He swallowed a bite and reached for a napkin. "Actually, pretty well. I think I have about half of what I need, maybe a little more."

"But time is running out," Stacie said. "So we have to help."

"What can we do?" Megan asked. "You know I don't have any money. What I have is a pile of school loans to pay off."

"We know you're a pauper. But maybe one of us knows someone who can help."

"What about some of the bigger churches in town?" Megan suggested.

"Good idea," Dillon said. "But I already tried them. Several of them are willing to contribute monthly to the renovation costs and ongoing expenses, but they don't want to be involved in buying the property."

"I may know someone," Brad said, licking his fingertips.

Stacie gave him a scolding look. "Why haven't you said something sooner?"

"Because it's a long shot and I didn't want to get everyone's hopes up. I was hoping Dillon would be able to raise the money."

"Spill the beans!" Stacie insisted.

"There's a banker I could talk to about a loan."

Dillon groaned and shook his head. "I've already tried the banks. No one believes the camp could generate enough income to meet the mortgage payment."

Brad tilted his head thoughtfully. "Well, this guy has been known to take some unusual risks. He doesn't always believe the number crunchers."

"Brad, if I were a banker, I wouldn't give me a mortgage," Dillon said flatly. "I'm no financial whiz, but I'm smart enough to see that a guy living on my salary cannot afford this property."

"But the property would be its own collateral. The worst that could happen is that the bank would repossess the property."

"That's a pretty gruesome picture," Megan said.

"Not any more gruesome than seeing it sold to someone else because we didn't try absolutely everything."

"Well, okay," Dillon conceded. "It can't hurt to ask, even if it does make us look like complete fools."

"I'll call him tomorrow and set up a meeting." Brad said definitively. "Then it's up to you to win him over with your charm."

From there the conversation digressed to what major renovations Dillon thought were needed and what they would cost. Gradually the two pizzas disappeared, and left in their place were greasy paper napkins and assorted empty pop cans. The evening wore on and the talk wound down.

Eventually Megan was again alone with her cat.

"It just might happen, Franklin," she said softly. "I just might get what I want from all of this."

She squeezed her eyes shut and added, "Please, Lord, Dillon is new to You, but he would use that place for Your glory. Please let him find the money he needs."

twenty

"There, I think that's straight now."

Megan stood back to assess the details of the bride standing nervously before her. Stacie's white satin dress had a sequined bodice with a scooped neckline and long sleeves. The skirt, overlaid with delicate lace, billowed out from her slender waist to a scalloped hemline. The matching lace in the veil hung over her rich coppery hair but did not hide its luster.

"You look like you stepped out of a fairy tale," Megan told Stacie.

Stacie laughed. "Only a romantic like you would say something like that."

Megan smiled; she supposed that was true. "Have you seen your groom today?"

Stacie shook her head. "No, we decided not to see each other until the ceremony."

"Well, he couldn't ask for a more beautiful bride."

"You look pretty good yourself."

Megan's dress, made from a silky blue fabric that matched the shade of the candles and Stacie's flowers, draped off her shoulders and hips in a way that showed off the fine figure usually lost in her loose comfortable clothes. The full sleeves gathered into tidy cuffs at her wrists, and the back of the skirt had just enough extra length to create a regal air when she walked.

"Where are the others?" Stacie asked, suddenly anxious about the absence of her other bridesmaids.

"Relax, they're already here. They've been dressed for

a long time and wanted to get out of this room for a while."

Megan gestured around the tiny room, furnished only with a small wooden table that needed painting and a pair of worn out gold velvet chairs. As a concession to the brides who used the room, a full length mirror was attached to the back of the door.

Stacie fanned herself with one hand. "I thought it was just my nerves that made this room feel so small. I can hardly breathe."

"You're gonna be fine, Stace," Megan lightly touched Stacie's arm to reassure her. "It won't be long now until all your careful planning will pay off. It'll be the perfect wedding."

Stacie nodded and sighed. "I've been planning for this for so long. But you know, part of me just wants it over with!"

"You're just nervous. Try to relax."

"I wish I could sit down, but that would be more trouble than it's worth." She was wadding up a tissue until it was nearly shredded.

"Here, let me touch up your lipstick." Megan set about adding the finishing touches to Stacie's makeup, which gave Stacie something to concentrate on and seemed to calm her down.

"The light in here is terrible. I hope I'm not overdoing your lips."

"I can't wait to see what *your* wedding is like," Stacie said as they stood eyeball to eyeball.

Megan snapped the cap back on the lipstick. "Rick wants to get married outside. But I worry about rain. That would ruin everything."

"I assume you're going to get married here, in St. Mary's."

"I'm sure we will. We have an appointment to talk to

the pastor next week."

"You seem so confident about it all. Doesn't it scare you to think about getting married?"

Megan's eyes widened. "Am I supposed to be scared?"

"I am."

"But you and Brad are perfect for each other."

"There you go with your romantic notions again. I'm sure we haven't had our last disagreement."

"Disagreeing doesn't mean you don't belong together." Megan zipped the small cosmetic bag shut and set it down on the wooden table, turning away from Stacie as she did so. "I know Rick and I seem very different to you, maybe too different."

"Oh, Megan, I didn't mean—"

"It's okay, Stace, really it is. I know Rick and I are different. But down deep, we want the same things: work that means something, family, love."

"Megan, I hope you don't think that I don't like Rick. I think he's great! I'm sorry if I've been acting like a mother hen."

"This is a whole new era for us, isn't it, Stacie?"

Stacie nodded thoughtfully. "For six years, we've been practically inseparable. Now we're getting married and you're moving away."

"One thing at a time!" Megan said, lightening the mood. "The immediate problem is whether your flower girl is actually going to go down the aisle."

Stacie rolled her eyes. "I couldn't believe it when she wouldn't practice last night. She insists she already knows how to do it and doesn't need to practice. But I have no idea what she's going to do today."

"Did you hear from Dillon yet?"

"Yes," Stacie answered with a careful nod. "He called early this morning to repeat his offer to walk me down the aisle."

"Why didn't you take him up on it? It might be nice to have someone to lean on."

"I've been on my own since I was nineteen. There's something symbolic about going to Brad on my own." Stacie gently pushed her veil over her shoulder. "But it was sweet of Dillon to offer."

"I almost hate to ask, but did he say anything about the loan?"

Stacie gasped and put her hand to her lips. "I can't believe I forgot to tell you. Yes—they got it! Jenna told me just a few minutes ago."

"She's been acting like it was a sure thing all along."

"I know. She wants to help with everything that needs to be done." Stacie carefully shrugged one shoulder. "I guess it shouldn't surprise us. She lived out there and worked with Mrs. Barrows all last summer."

"When I stop to think about it, she has more reason to be attached to the camp than we do."

A sharp rap on the door interrupted them. The church wedding director stuck her head in and said, "It's time, ladies. Are you ready?"

Megan looked at Stacie with a question in her eyes. Stacie pressed her lips together and nodded.

"Ready," Megan answered.

"The flowers are in the narthex," the wedding director said efficiently. "The other bridesmaids are up there, too. Megan, you pick up the back of the bride's dress. Be especially careful going around corners and up the stairs."

She turned to lead the way out, muttering. "I don't know why they don't put the bride's room closer to the sanctuary."

Megan and Stacie looked at each other and smiled in amusement.

"Here we go," said Megan, bending to pick up Stacie's six-foot train. "Have you got a tissue?"

Stacie held out the shredded wad in her hand.

Megan clucked her tongue. "That's pretty pitiful. Get a fresh one and tuck it in your sleeve."

Stacie obeyed without question, and they began the ascent to the sanctuary level.

In the narthex were the other bridesmaids and Brad's four-year-old niece, the flower girl. The soothing tones of the organ wafted toward them. From the door at the back of the sanctuary, Megan got just a glimpse of the full sanctuary.

"Looks like the seats are all sold out," she said, making Stacie smile.

At the cue of the wedding director, the organ swelled into the processional music and the first bridesmaid began her journey. She kept her pace even and smooth, and Megan hoped she would do as well. The candelabras with the fourteen perfectly matched blue candles stood on the platform. A few steps lower, on elegant carved stands, were the baskets of fresh flowers. Brad and his three groomsmen were soberly lined up on the right side, their hands hanging straight at their sides just as they had been adamantly instructed at the rehearsal.

When the first bridesmaid was halfway down the aisle, the second one followed. Then it would be Megan's turn, and soon the picture would be complete. She glanced over at Stacie, who was already teary-eyed and forcibly swallowed the lump in her throat.

"Go!" whispered the wedding director, nudging Megan's elbow.

Although she knew it was loud, Megan was having a hard time hearing the music. Where was the beat? Was she supposed to be moving her left foot or her right?

Finally, she fell into a rhythm that she thought was right.

The other bridesmaids had reached the front and perfectly executed their turns to face the congregation. Megan blinked her eyes and drew her mouth out to a smile as Brad caught her eye and winked at her. Finally, she reached the front and saw the masking tape X marking her spot. She stepped on it and pivoted perfectly, standing in alignment with the rest of the wedding party.

Without planning to, she scanned the congregation until her eyes settled on Rick, seated halfway back on the bride's side. Their eyes locked and her nerves steadied. Two rows behind Rick, she saw Dillon and Jenna sitting together. They had been brought together by their work at the camp; somehow, right then, they looked like they belonged together. Megan blinked and focused her eyes again on the wedding procession.

The moment of truth had come. What would the flower girl do? Megan glanced back at Stacie, who stood back from the center doors at the rear of the sanctuary, and then focused on the little girl. Meticulously, the girl pulled one petal at a time from her basket and dropped it in front of her. A thin delicate trail formed behind her as she made slow but steady progress toward the front.

Megan could hear the muffled amusement of the other bridesmaids as they also watched. Megan was sure Stacie had envisioned that the girl would joyously toss whole flowers on the white runner, but she had to admit the petal dropping was cute. At last the job was done, and the little girl came and stood stiffly beside Megan.

The organ swelled once again and the congregation rose on cue. All heads turned toward the center aisle as Stacie entered the back of the sanctuary.

She's absolutely beautiful, Megan thought to herself. *This is not the end of an era; it is the beginning of something wonderful—for both of us.* She looked over at Rick again, and blushed when she saw that his eyes were fixed on her, not on the bride.

Megan had promised herself she would leave the crying to the bride, but as she watched her friend floating down the aisle toward the front of the church, a tear of happiness escaped and slid down her cheek.

A Letter To Our Readers

Dear Reader:

In order that we might better contribute to your reading enjoyment, we would appreciate your taking a few minutes to respond to the following questions. When completed, please return to the following:

Rebecca Germany, Editor
Heartsong Presents
P.O. Box 719
Uhrichsville, Ohio 44683

1. Did you enjoy reading *Between Love and Loyalty*?
   ☐ Very much. I would like to see more books
      by this author!
   ☐ Moderately
      I would have enjoyed it more if _____

   _____

2. Are you a member of *Heartsong Presents*? Yes   No
   If no, where did you purchase this book? _____

   _____

3. What influenced your decision to purchase
   this book? (Circle those that apply.)

Cover	Back cover copy
Title	Friends
Publicity	Other _____

4. On a scale from 1 (poor) to 10 (superior), please rate the following elements.

    ___Heroine   ___Plot

    ___Hero   ___Inspirational theme

    ___Setting   ___Secondary characters

5. What settings would you like to see covered in *Heartsong Presents* books?

_____

_____

6. What are some inspirational themes you would like to see treated in future books?_____

_____

_____

7. Would you be interested in reading other *Heartsong Presents* titles?   Yes   No

8. Please circle your age range:

| Under 18 | 18-24 | 25-34 |
| 35-45 | 46-55 | Over 55 |

9. How many hours per week do you read? _____

Name _____

Occupation _____

Address _____

City _____ State _____ Zip _____

····· Heart♥ng ·········

ROMANCE IS CHEAPER BY THE DOZEN!

Any 12 *Heartsong Presents* titles for only $26.95 *

Buy any assortment of twelve *Heartsong Presents* titles and save 25% off of the already discounted price of $2.95 each!

*plus $1.00 shipping and handling per order and sales tax where applicable.

HEARTSONG PRESENTS TITLES AVAILABLE NOW:

__HP 1 A TORCH FOR TRINITY, *Colleen L. Reece*
__HP 2 WILDFLOWER HARVEST, *Colleen L. Reece*
__HP 3 RESTORE THE JOY, *Sara Mitchell*
__HP 4 REFLECTIONS OF THE HEART, *Sally Laity*
__HP 5 THIS TREMBLING CUP, *Marlene Chase*
__HP 6 THE OTHER SIDE OF SILENCE, *Marlene Chase*
__HP 7 CANDLESHINE, *Colleen L. Reece*
__HP 8 DESERT ROSE, *Colleen L. Reece*
__HP 9 HEARTSTRINGS, *Irene B. Brand*
__HP10 SONG OF LAUGHTER, *Lauraine Snelling*
__HP11 RIVER OF FIRE, *Jacquelyn Cook*
__HP13 PASSAGE OF THE HEART, *Kjersti Hoff Baez*
__HP14 A MATTER OF CHOICE, *Susannah Hayden*
__HP15 WHISPERS ON THE WIND, *Maryn Langer*
__HP16 SILENCE IN THE SAGE, *Colleen L. Reece*
__HP17 LLAMA LADY, *VeraLee Wiggins*
__HP18 ESCORT HOMEWARD, *Eileen M. Berger*
__HP19 A PLACE TO BELONG, *Janelle Jamison*
__HP20 SHORES OF PROMISE, *Kate Blackwell*
__HP21 GENTLE PERSUASION, *Veda Boyd Jones*
__HP22 INDY GIRL, *Brenda Bancroft*
__HP23 GONE WEST, *Kathleen Karr*
__HP24 WHISPERS IN THE WILDERNESS, *Colleen L. Reece*
__HP25 REBAR, *Mary Carpenter Reid*
__HP26 MOUNTAIN HOUSE, *Mary Louise Colln*
__HP27 BEYOND THE SEARCHING RIVER, *Jacquelyn Cook*
__HP28 DAKOTA DAWN, *Lauraine Snelling*
__HP29 FROM THE HEART, *Sara Mitchell*
__HP30 A LOVE MEANT TO BE, *Brenda Bancroft*
__HP31 DREAM SPINNER, *Sally Laity*
__HP32 THE PROMISED LAND, *Kathleen Karr*
__HP33 SWEET SHELTER, *VeraLee Wiggins*
__HP34 UNDER A TEXAS SKY, *Veda Boyd Jones*
__HP35 WHEN COMES THE DAWN, *Brenda Bancroft*
__HP36 THE SURE PROMISE, *JoAnn A. Grote*
__HP37 DRUMS OF SHELOMOH, *Yvonne Lehman*
__HP38 A PLACE TO CALL HOME, *Eileen M. Berger*
__HP39 RAINBOW HARVEST, *Norene Morris*
__HP40 PERFECT LOVE, *Janelle Jamison*
__HP41 FIELDS OF SWEET CONTENT, *Norma Jean Lutz*
__HP42 SEARCH FOR TOMORROW, *Mary Hawkins*

(If ordering from this page, please remember to include it with the order form.)

·········· Presents ··········

Great Inspirational Romance at a Great Price!
Heartsong Presents books are inspirational romances in contemporary and historical settings, designed to give you an enjoyable, spirit-lifting reading experience. You can choose from 73 wonderfully written titles from some of today's best authors like Colleen L. Reece, Brenda Bancroft, Janelle Jamison, and many others.

When ordering quantities less than twelve, above titles are $2.95 each.

SEND TO: Heartsong Presents Reader's Service
        P.O. Box 719, Uhrichsville, Ohio 44683

Please send me the items checked above. I am enclosing $_____
(please add $1.00 to cover postage per order. OH add 6.5% tax. PA and
NJ add 6%.). Send check or money order, no cash or C.O.D.s, please.
        To place a credit card order, call 1-800-847-8270.

NAME _____

ADDRESS _____

CITY/STATE_____ZIP _____
                                            HPS APRIL

LOVE A GREAT LOVE STORY?

Introducing Heartsong Presents —
Your Inspirational Book Club

Heartsong Presents Christian romance reader's service will provide you with four never before published romance titles every month! In fact, your books will be mailed to you at the same time advance copies are sent to book reviewers. You'll preview each of these new and unabridged books before they are released to the general public.

These books are filled with the kind of stories you have been longing for—stories of courtship, chivalry, honor, and virtue. Strong characters and riveting plot lines will make you want to read on and on. Romance is not dead, and each of these romantic tales will remind you that Christian faith is still the vital ingredient in an intimate relationship filled with true love and honest devotion.

Sign up today to receive your first set. Send no money now. We'll bill you only $9.97 post-paid with your shipment. Then every month you'll automatically receive the latest four "hot off the press" titles for the same low post-paid price of $9.97. That's a savings of 50% off the $4.95 cover price. When you consider the exaggerated shipping charges of other book clubs, your savings are even greater!

THERE IS NO RISK—you may cancel at any time without obligation. And if you aren't completely satisfied with any selection, return it for an immediate refund.

TO JOIN, just complete the coupon below, mail it today, and get ready for hours of wholesome entertainment.

Now you can curl up, relax, and enjoy some great reading full of the warmhearted spirit of romance.

——— Curl up with Heartsong! ———

YES! Sign me up for Heartsong!

NEW MEMBERSHIPS WILL BE SHIPPED IMMEDIATELY!
Send no money now. We'll bill you only $9.97 post-paid with your first shipment of four books. Or for faster action, call toll free 1-800-847-8270.

NAME _____

ADDRESS _____

CITY _____ STATE / ZIP _____

MAIL TO: HEARTSONG / P.O. Box 719 Uhrichsville, Ohio 44683
YES II

Self-controlled, logical Megan was surprised by her attraction to Rick.

Reluctantly Megan turned to put her key in the door. "Do you want to come in for coffee?"

Her heart pounded while she waited for his answer.

"I'd love to, Megan, but it's late, you know. I'll be in enough hot water with Carol for keeping you out this late on a school night."

Megan leaned against the door and nodded at his common sense. "I had a really good time, Rick," she said quietly, looking down at the keys in her hands.

"Me too. I hope we can do it again."

This time she was nodding enthusiasm. "I'd like that."

"I hope you'll like this, too."

Rick caught Megan by the chin and tilted her face toward his. When his lips came down on hers, she knew this was what she had been waiting for all evening. She willingly leaned into his chest to return his kiss.

SUSANNAH HAYDEN is the pen name of a versatile and gifted author of fiction and biography for both adults and children. Her recent inspirational romances include the popular *Summer's Wind Blowing, Spring Waters Rushing,* and *A Matter of Choice.*

Books by Susannah Hayden

HEARTSONG PRESENTS
HP14—A Matter of Choice

ROMANCE READER—TWO BOOKS IN ONE
RR9—Summer's Wind Blowing & Spring Waters Rushing

Don't miss out on any of our super romances. Write to us at the following address for information on our newest releases and club information.

Heartsong Presents Reader's Service
P.O. Box 719
Uhrichsville, OH 44683